REUNITED WITH HER HOT-SHOT SURGEON

AMY RUTTAN

MILLS & BOON

First published in Great Britain 2020
by Mills & Boon, an imprint of HarperCollins*Publishers*
1 London Bridge Street, London, SE1 9GF

Large Print edition 2021

© 2020 Amy Ruttan

ISBN: 978-0-263-28754-7

MIX
Paper from
responsible sources
FSC™ C007454

This book is produced from independently certified FSC™ paper to ensure responsible forest management. For more information visit www.harpercollins.co.uk/green.

Printed and bound in Great Britain
by CPI Group (UK) Ltd, Croydon, CR0 4YY

For Dianne.
Thank you for being so kind
when I needed support,
especially when I was a new author.
You won't be forgotten.

PROLOGUE

"You don't have to do this."

"I have to. It was the plan." Pearl continued to pack her bags, fighting back the tears stinging her eyes. She wasn't going to cry in front of him.

"Why?" Calum asked, confused.

"We agreed to get married because of the baby. The baby is gone, so I'm going to continue with my plans. I'm going to take the job I was offered after residency." She hoped her voice didn't shake as she packed.

Calum had always said that they'd get married for the baby. After they finished their residency, around the time Pearl had gotten pregnant, he'd been offered a job here in San Francisco. Pearl hadn't, but there was a job in New York City. She'd originally turned it down because she was pregnant, but now that was a moot point.

She had always had reservations about getting married. He knew her parents, had met her mother, so he got why she didn't want to get married. Or at least understood why there was no point now the baby was gone.

When she'd fallen pregnant Pearl had been scared. Marriage had seemed like a safety net. It had seemed like the right thing to do at the time.

She loved Calum, but when they'd started this relationship over a year ago they had both made it clear from the start that their careers came first.

"Pearl, we can still stay together."

She stopped packing and stared at him. She wanted to believe Calum, but she knew how he felt about marriage, too. And it was hard to look at him, because she still loved him, so she looked away, because if she looked at him he might convince her to stay, and just prolong eventual heartbreak.

"So I stay and we do what? We still get married?" she asked.

He hesitated. "Eventually…"

Pearl sighed. "It's best I go. That job I was offered in New York City is still waiting for me."

"So that's it? You're taking that high-profile job? The one your father suggested you take?" There was derision in his voice.

She didn't give a lick about the fact it was high-profile or paid well. She needed to get away. The pain was too much. Everywhere reminded her of the baby, how she was almost happy. How she almost had her happily-ever-after and the family she wanted. The family she always longed for growing up with toxic parents. Parents she could never please. The only good times in her life had been with her late grandmother and Calum.

But she and Calum had both wanted very different career paths when they first met. She wasn't going to hold him back any longer.

"You don't have to run off and leave just because we don't have to get married," Calum said.

"Why? We both had plans for our career. You don't have to marry me now. I know that you were doing it because of some sense of duty, but there's no point now—the baby is gone. You're off the hook. Me leaving or you leaving for work was going to be the eventual and natural end to this relationship." She continued to pack and tried not to cry. She didn't want the tears that were burning her eyes to fall.

She wanted to keep those tears to herself. She'd learned to keep them to herself. They were hers and she wouldn't burden Calum with them.

She wanted a family. She wanted happiness,

but that was a dream she'd learned to give up long ago.

"You really think that I wanted to marry you because of some outdated sense of duty?" he asked hotly.

"Didn't you?"

"Yes. At first, I suppose, but..." He trailed off and rubbed the back of his neck, not saying anything else.

"Why else would we eventually get married then? You told me you didn't want a family when we both got together. We agreed on that. So why else?"

His expression hardened. "Things changed this past year, Pearl."

"What changed? Nothing changed for me except the baby and that's gone. It's back to the way it was."

"Is it?"

"Yes." Only she was lying. She was giving him an out.

She was giving herself an out. She was too afraid to continue. She knew what happened when surgeons married, when one was forced to change career trajectory for another.

She knew from painful experience what happened. Calum would eventually resent her for holding him back.

And she'd resent him.

Are you sure?

"I've accepted the job, Calum. I've got to go." She zipped up her luggage.

"Fine. Then go. It's clear where your priorities lie."

He left, slamming the door, making her cringe.

This was for the best.

Although, she wasn't so sure.

CHAPTER ONE

Five years later

BREATHE.

Dr. Pearl Henderson took a deep breath, but it didn't do much to calm her nerves. She was perspiring and cursed herself inwardly for wearing a sweater. She'd forgotten that October in San Francisco was much milder than New York City.

She'd been on the East Coast for far too long. She'd grown accustomed to cooler and cold New York City falls and winters, and the humid, steamy summers. Although she had always longed for California.

It's your fault for leaving.

Pearl had been so scared about what could happen if she and Calum had stayed together that she had left. She was a damn fine surgeon and sports doctor, but she never took chances.

Except now.

She was back in California and San Francisco.

She was back to see Calum.

The grip on her briefcase was digging into her palm and she closed her eyes, trying to ground herself, trying to ease the stress she was feeling being back here in San Francisco. At this hospital. The place where she'd started her career as a surgeon.

The place that held a piece of her broken heart.

A place that still haunted her, even after five years. She'd always wanted to come back, but she never knew how. She was one of the top sports injury doctors on the eastern seaboard, but it wasn't enough.

Because you miss him.

Pearl shook away that thought. She couldn't let herself think like that, even if there was a bit of truth in it. It wasn't Calum who had brought her back to San Francisco, it was her new job as head physician that brought her back here.

You're lying to yourself.

She took another deep breath, taking in the salty, crisp air as she straightened her back and held her head up high. It was going to be hard to see Dr. Calum Munro again—it would be brutal. Ending their relationship and walking away from the only man she cared for had broken her heart, but she'd had no choice.

When they got together Calum had made it clear that he didn't want to get married and she had agreed. They both had goals, aspirations, and marriage wasn't one of his.

He deserved to be free. It would take every ounce of strength to face him again, but she was a professional and her patient needed her to act on his behalf. Her employer, the San Francisco Bridgers, a new team part of the NFL, had hired her to do this.

To save their potential star player. To give George a fighting chance in the face of a brutal cancer diagnosis. A career-ending diagnosis.

The Bridgers' newest player had an osteosarcoma that only Dr. Calum Munro could handle. He may have turned down the team initially, without looking at the chart, but she wasn't about to let his busy schedule, his wait list, put this life in jeopardy. George had worked hard all his life and he deserved a chance at his dream. He'd only got to play a couple of games, he had his whole career ahead of him and now cancer.

Someone deserved to have a shot at their dreams. Pearl certainly hadn't had a shot at hers.

That had been taken from her; she hadn't known what she had had until it was gone. She only hoped Calum had forgiven her and that he'd see her.

Pearl didn't take him for the kind of man that would hold a grudge. Not that there should be one. She certainly didn't blame him for the way their relationship had ended.

Pearl had been the one to end it. With the baby gone there was no reason to continue and she was keenly reminded that anything good in her life didn't ever work out. Except her work. And that was the only thing she could rely on. Even her own body had failed her in a way for not being able to hold on to her baby.

The thought of her loss made her eyes sting, but she couldn't cry.

"Surgeons don't cry," her mother had once said. "Never show your weakness or let anyone walk all over you. Your tears disappoint me, Pearl. Do you ever see me cry over your father holding me back? No, because surgeons don't cry."

Her mother's harsh words still echoed in her head. The only time she was ever allowed to be herself, where her tears were comforted, was with her grandmother.

After her mother shamed her, she didn't cry in front of anyone anymore.

Not even Calum.

Pearl took another deep calming breath and headed inside the Hospital for Special Surgery, where Calum worked, where they had both started together as residents. Where her career life had flourished, but her personal life had started to crumble.

You can do this.

She walked into the main lobby of the hospital. Nothing had changed and the moment she stepped inside, it was like she'd never left.

It felt like home. All the old memories came back. The friendships she had made, the triumphs she'd had, the lives she had saved.

This place had taught her everything she knew. This is where she'd belonged. This is where she fell in love.

She had thrived here and been welcomed, unlike the place she had grown up with parents constantly fighting.

With parents who were never pleased with her or themselves.

Only this wasn't her home. This was a hospital. It was a building. It was just like every other hospital she'd worked in since and she didn't belong here anymore.

She had to stay focused. Pearl found where Calum's office was. She'd already called ahead and knew that he wasn't on call. He didn't have any clinics and his rounds would be over by now.

He should be in his office.

He couldn't turn her down. If he was the same man that she had known five years ago he'd rise to the challenge of George's case.

She was sure of that.

Are you so sure?

Yes. She was sure. Calum liked difficult cases. Just like she did.

Which is why they had become fast friends in residency. They had both strived to tackle the challenges and save lives.

They had both worked hard.

Calum had been the only one to understand her.

Even though her mother always said surgeons couldn't be friends or lovers. And her mother should know thanks to her toxic marriage with Pearl's father.

"It's competitive," her mother had said. "It doesn't work. The only thing that works is surgery. That's all that matters—being the best at your job."

And her father had said the same. Only Calum had been different.

He was different.

Was he?

Her mother swore she'd loved her father once, but it changed. Her mother's career was put on hold when she had Pearl, and her mother loathed him and Pearl.

So who knew where Calum and she would be if she hadn't lost their baby. If they had gone through with the marriage.

She got onto the elevator and headed to the orthopedic oncology floor. The hospital hadn't changed much. She and Calum had spent a lot of time on this floor when they were residents under the late great Dr. Chin, who'd taught them everything they knew.

After getting off the elevator, she bypassed the main reception area and headed straight for the office down at the end of the hall. Each step she took down that long hall felt like an eternity. Her feet felt like lead and her pulse thundered in her ears. The door was open and she could see him at his desk, his back to her. The ginger hair she loved so much had a few grays in it and it was shorter than she remembered.

It had been slightly longer then and she remembered brushing the curls off his face to kiss him. Her heart skipped a beat remembering that. He hadn't changed a bit. She had thought that time would've made this easier and she had been wrong.

Everything came flooding back to her in that instant.

Every touch.

Every shared laugh.

Every kiss.

It overwhelmed her so much her heart hammered and she couldn't speak.

So she just hovered in the doorway, not sure what she should do. Calum turned around, as if sensing that someone was watching him, and his eyes widened. "Pearl?" he asked.

"Yes," she answered nervously, finally finding her voice. Her tongue was no longer sticking to the roof of her mouth. She cleared her throat, keeping her emotions in check. "It's been a long time."

The warmth that was once in those blue eyes that she so loved dissipated quickly, his expression hardening. "Has it?" And without asking her anything further he returned to his work.

Okay. So apparently he did hold something of a grudge.

It hurt, but what did she expect? She was used to indifference and formality. This is what her mother told her would happen. She was prepared for this. Only…it still hurt. She had hoped Calum was different. Apparently, she was wrong.

"Calum," she said firmly. She wasn't going to be swayed or pushed aside. She was here for her patient.

That wasn't why she was back.

"There's nothing to say, Pearl. I don't want to talk about the past. You're five years too late for that."

"I didn't come all this way to rehash the past. I came here to talk about a case."

"I have a wait list. I don't have time to take on cases," he said. "There are other surgeons in this hospital that I'm sure have room."

"You are seriously holding on to the past?" she asked, pulling the door closed behind her.

His eyes narrowed as he turned around. "I'm

not holding on to the past. I'm stating a fact. I'm swamped and I don't have time to take on some athlete who has some injury that's preventing him from making millions as a…quarterback."

"Linebacker," Pearl said offhandedly.

"Whatever," Calum responded dryly. "There are other surgeons."

"How did you know it's for a football player? Is that why you turned the case down without looking at the chart?"

"I know you were hired as a physician for a sports team in New York. Everyone knows you're the top of your field. Congrats on that, by the way," he said dryly.

Was he jealous?

Calum had always told her he wanted a big career. That was why he had become a doctor.

She didn't want to believe it, but his apparent jealously seemed to prove otherwise.

"I'm based here in California now." She pulled out her patient's file. "And it's not some injury. I can handle any surgery for an injury. It's an osteosarcoma and a brutal one. I know that you have the best success rate for saving the leg, for saving the bone. This young man has worked so hard through college, scholarships and odd jobs just to get here, and then has had this side-line him."

He turned back to look at her. "An osteosar-coma?"

"Yes. I can't help him and you're the best, or so I've been told. This player came from nothing to become a superstar. He's young and deserves a fighting chance."

Calum's expression softened and she knew she was getting to him. Calum had worked so hard to get through medical school. He had had it harder than others and she knew that even though this young man had signed a six-figure contract, that the rough start in life, the deter-mination the young man had put forth, might just soften Calum's heart a bit. It always had in the past.

When they'd been working on patients, he'd always take the pro bono cases.

Always.

Though she was worried he'd say no to the team again because she was working for them and because his father was an investor for the Bridgers. She knew Calum didn't have the best relationship with his father, but a young man's life was at stake. And if Calum was still the man she remembered, he would do what he could for George.

It was that softness she knew laid deep inside, that drew her to him.

He flipped open the file and leaned back in his chair, reading it.

Pearl stood there, her pulse racing, and she wondered if she really still did know Calum. Had he changed in five years? Would he help? If she believed what her parents had always told her, then no, he wouldn't. He would hold a grudge like her parents did.

Calum wasn't like that. He always wanted to help others. She knew that about him.

Did you ever really know him, though?

Pearl was confident she knew the type of surgeon he was. His compassion and his drive to be the best were what had drawn her to him in the first place.

Even though she didn't want to date or have a relationship after growing up through her parents' awful marriage, Calum was so different. He had been a breath of fresh air in her stagnant, emotionless life.

He had brought color to her dark, bleak world.

Pearl had grown up in a house where her parents fought, cheated and blamed each other for their failures.

Her parents were constantly trying to outdo one another, until finally in her last year of medical school they got divorced. Finally, there was no arguing. Although, there was really nothing anymore. There was no home to go home to during school breaks.

Her mother was bitter and angry. Her father started a new life and a new family with a younger woman.

Their hate for each other steeled Pearl's resolve to never date someone she worked with.

Until she met Calum.

He was a high achiever, and so was she, but he understood her unhappy childhood.

He got it.

And they bonded. She was drawn to his light in spite of the darkness of her past.

He was comforting.

He was home.

Then one night, one foolish drunken night, she couldn't resist that strong attraction, the need she had for Calum, and one thing led to another and another, and that had ended up in eventual heartache.

Heartache she wasn't too keen on ever experiencing again. She was going to make sure of that.

"This isn't good," he said gently, still focused on the file.

"No. It's not. Can I sit down?" she asked. He nodded and she took a seat on the other side of his desk.

Calum set down the file and scrubbed a hand over his face. "Look, I'm sorry. I didn't know that it was a cancer and I didn't know that it was this bad. I thought it was just another sports team trying to woo me to leave the hospital. I thought it was an injury and I thought any surgeon could handle it."

"I could handle an injury myself. I would've just asked the chief of surgery for special privileges to work at the hospital. This is something else. Something I can't handle. I need help."

Calum nodded. "I'm sorry for this young man—this is rough."

"Can you make time to see him? There's no one else I'd rather have on the case."

A strange expression crossed his face. "Why me?"

"You're a great surgeon, Calum, and I thought from one friend to another—"

"We're not friends, Pearl," he stated firmly. "Colleagues on this case, but if I take this patient on, he's my patient. I don't need your assistance."

It was another slap in the face. It stung, but she was prepared for that reaction. The only thing she was not prepared to do was step aside when it came to her patient. She couldn't.

Pearl straightened her spine. "He's my patient, too. I'm responsible for everyone on that team and I will be with him every step of the way. You don't know him or the treatments he's had. I won't back down when it comes to my patient. I'll treat you cordially, since you stated we're not friends, but I won't be pushed aside."

"Fine."

She was relieved, but she hid that from him. Like she hid so many other emotions. Calum could be just as stubborn as her. He never really liked to be backed into a corner, that much she remembered from their days as residents. He wouldn't step down if he felt it was the right thing to do. Something else she admired about him.

Part of her wanted to pull back, let him handle this case. That way she could keep her distance and not let him affect her. Already being near him was dredging up all these old feelings and memories she thought she'd locked away. She wasn't going to be bullied out of this. George was her patient and she had been with him right from the start. Right from when the San Francisco Bridgers had signed him from college, up to his injury after his third game, until his diagnosis.

George lived far from his home in Philadelphia and his mother was on her way out to see him, but she had other kids at home and Pearl felt bad that George was on his own. She made it her mission to take care of him and she wasn't going to be pushed aside because of Calum.

"Thank you," she said.

His expression softened. "You're welcome, but I do expect some compensation."

"The team will pay you."

"I know that, but for privileges to *my* hospital I want you to take some of my caseload." He grinned and there was a twinkle in his eye.

"What? I don't have time for that!"

A smile tugged at the corners of his mouth. "I think you can make time. I am making time for your patient."

Heat bloomed in her cheeks.

He was right.

And it honestly secretly thrilled her to do surgical work again. Most of her surgeries as a sports doctor involved knee replacements or torn ligaments. Sports type of injuries. It would be nice to do a rotation on the trauma floor. To work on a variety of different cases.

Pearl stood up, yanking up her briefcase swiftly. "You have a deal, Dr. Munro. Thank you for seeing my patient. When can I bring him in?"

"I'm glad to hear it," he said. "You can call me Calum, you know."

"Why? We're not friends, you said so yourself."

"I didn't mean to insult you before. I was just surprised to see you standing there again after all this time." He ran his hand through his ginger hair and sighed. "It's been a long time."

She smiled. "You didn't insult me. And, yes, it's been a long time."

"You don't need to be so formal. It feels weird having you call me Dr. Munro."

"You said you wanted to keep it professional."

"I know. Again, it was a shock. You haven't changed at all."

Her heart skipped a beat. "Neither have you."

And he hadn't. Not really. She thought five

years apart would've been enough time to lay the ghosts of her past to rest.

She was wrong.

"So when can I bring George in?" she asked, trying to ignore all the feelings he was stirring up in her. She had to put an end to this conversation and put some distance between them.

"How about you bring him in this afternoon? Say around four? Does that work."

"It does."

"And Pearl, try to relax. I'm sorry for what I said. It was just… It was a shock to see you standing in my door."

She relaxed a bit. She understood that. It was a shock to see him, too, but she wasn't going to let him know that. She had to keep her distance, though it would be hard working with him. She was drawn to him. She'd always been.

Even though she knew she was here to see Calum, she wasn't mentally prepared to see him again. She thought she had prepared enough, but seeing him there, sitting at his desk, brought it all back.

The night she left him. It was still fresh in her mind, haunting her. She had hated herself for leaving. Though it had been the right thing to do.

Had it?

Pearl shook that memory from her mind. "I'll see you at four."

"Sounds good."

Pearl opened the door and left his office. Her hands were shaking and her pulse was racing. She wasn't quite ready for the effect that Dr. Calum Munro still had on her. And she was going to make sure that she had full control over it. She wasn't going to risk her heart for anything.

Not even if it wanted to.

Calum leaned back in his chair, trying to process what had happened. He had no idea that Dr. Pearl Henderson had come back to San Francisco. He had no idea that she worked for the San Francisco Bridgers. Maybe if he had known...

Would that have really changed your mind?

It might have.

When the Bridgers came to him he thought it was his father reaching out, trying to get a freebie. His father only wanted him when Calum could give him something.

After years of trying to please his father, he had learned no matter what he achieved, no matter what he did, he'd never gain the attention or respect of Grayson Munro.

So he had given up trying and caring.

Calum had been approached by every major league team in San Francisco—and beyond— ever since he had won his major scientific achievement award, also known as the MSA, through his alma mater for his treatment in osteosarcoma. His practice blew up, but he just couldn't be lured by the money to be the exclusive doctor for a sports team. Not anymore.

When he first started out, Calum might have been tempted because he was sure it would have impressed his father, but when Pearl left he realized he couldn't live his life trying to impress others.

He loved the hospital. The hospital and his work were the only stable, constant things in his life.

He wanted to stay here.

He had researched and helped create that surgery so that he could help everyone with osteosarcoma, not just athletes. And, truth be told, he was a bit resentful of big teams like Bridgers.

It was a team out east that had lured away Pearl after they'd lost their baby. Even though he knew that's what she'd always wanted—to work as a sports doctor for a professional team—he still hated it.

Work was the most important thing to his father, and apparently it was to Pearl. Still, there was a part of him that didn't think that Pearl was all about the work—she was just using that as an excuse to run away. She had a tendency to shut out everyone when things got too hard. Bottle up her emotions when she became overwhelmed, like she was ashamed of them. He couldn't even remember ever seeing her cry before.

She certainly hadn't cried when they lost their baby.

She always tried to remain calm and collected, but he saw through that charade.

Are you sure it wasn't just an act?

There were moments during their time together, he really saw her. Saw her joy, her sorrow, her compassion and her vulnerability, but never her tears, so he had always suspected it was all a front.

No, he wasn't sure. Pearl had made it clear to him when they first met that she wasn't interested in dating anyone, especially not someone she worked with, and she wasn't interested in a traditional family.

Neither had he been, to be honest. His upbringing hadn't been the most wholesome and he had never really thought about having a family.

Ever.

He should've kept away from Pearl, but she was fun to be around. She was smart and sexy and after one foolish night one thing led to another and she was pregnant. For one golden moment in his life he had thought he could have the thing he had secretly wanted when he was growing up. He had been terrified of being a father, but he had wanted to try to be better than his father ever was. He wanted roots. His outlook had changed. He had wanted that family. He had wanted that tradition.

He had wanted Pearl.

He'd always wanted Pearl.

Then his world came crashing down and it was all taken from him. Instead of he and Pearl comforting each other over the loss of their child, she had left for that high-paying job she'd always aspired to and he had been left to grieve alone.

She had left him, just as his father had. His father had left and then his mother had died.

He had grieved for his mother alone and when Pearl left he had grieved alone for the child he had never known he'd wanted.

When he thought about being a husband and father, he thought he could be the man his father never was.

The kind of man his mother deserved. It's why he had never wanted a relationship. For so long he had known he couldn't commit. Until he'd met Pearl. He'd thought she was different.

It broke his heart, to carry that burden, when it had seemed like Pearl didn't care that their child was gone.

Only, he was used to being alone.

He should've known better.

No one stayed.

His sister, Sharon, left when she went to college and she never came back. His mother had to leave him alone to work and then she died.

Then Pearl left.

Pearl knew all this about him and she still left him, breaking his heart, but try as he might he couldn't let her go.

He could never get over her.

And that was his burden to bear.

He might never get over her, but he wasn't going to let her back in.

Calum had sworn that he would never forgive her, that he never wanted to see her again. But when he saw Pearl standing in that doorway, it was like time hadn't touched her. Like the last five years apart had never happened.

Her hair was still that deep, beautiful, rich color of chestnut mixed with red. Her brilliant blue eyes were just as mesmerizing as they were the day he looked up over a chart and saw her across the charge station with Dr. Chin.

And he remembered keenly the velvety softness of her lush pink lips, the way she tasted and the way she melted in his arms.

She was just as beautiful as he remembered, and all that anger that he felt about her leaving him dissipated. And he couldn't say no to her patient.

He might not want to work for a team exclusively, but he wasn't going to turn down a young man and ruin his chances at his dream because he was still angry that Pearl had left him.

He wasn't a monster. He wasn't like his father.

His father had only thought of their pocketbook. He worked constantly and had never helped out Calum. Calum had scrimped and saved, worked for scholarships, worked several jobs just to get himself an education. His father had had the money, but he wouldn't give him a dime.

He had kept it to himself. And Calum had never known why. It had bothered him, but now he didn't care. There was no excuse for that behavior.

Even when Calum's mother was broke and needed money to buy food to feed him and his sister, their father couldn't be bothered. His father had a facade of charm and made people trust him, believe in him, but he didn't care about anyone.

A narcissist. That's who his father was.

Pearl's not a narcissist.

He knew that. She really cared for her patients. She was tender and kind.

Compassionate and passionate about her work under the ice-queen exterior. It's why he was drawn to her. She seemed real when he spent his life surrounded by fake people.

Calum got up and followed after her—there were a few things he wanted to say to her. Pearl was almost at the end of the hall, where the main reception area was, and he didn't want to call out to her in front of his receptionist, who was a bit of a gossip and and had known him from his days as a resident, when he and Pearl had worked under Dr. Chin and learned all they could.

She remembered that they had been together, that there had been a baby, but he couldn't let her get away.

"Pearl, wait!" he called out.

She turned around, shocked. "Calum? Is there something wrong?"

He wanted to talk to her. He wanted to tell her how he felt that day she left, but he just couldn't get the words out and it made him angry that he couldn't.

There was so much he wanted to say to her but couldn't.

And there were things that he only wanted to keep to himself about that horrible night. Things that he felt that she didn't deserve to hear, but he still wanted her to know how her leaving had crushed him so completely.

For the last five years he'd been thinking of these things in his head, of what he would say if he saw her again. But now that he was presented with the opportunity, he couldn't get the words out.

He just couldn't do it.

She'd hurt him so badly, he wasn't going to share his heart with anyone again. Least of all with her.

"Why don't I come with you now to see George?" Really, he didn't want to go anywhere today. He had a lot of charts and paperwork to catch up on, but he couldn't think of any other reason to have chased her down the hall.

Like a fool. And that's what he was.

He was a fool chasing after her like he'd chased after his father.

"You want to come see him now?" she asked, confused.

"He must be in pain."

"He is," she said softly.

"Then it's better I go and see him now instead of forcing him to come here. I can do an initial exam there and then schedule him for regular clinic days. I'm sure you have the facilities to accommodate me."

"I do." She smiled, that warm genuine smile that not many people had seen when they were residents, but he'd seen it.

"You have a great smile you know," he'd said one day.

"What?" she had asked, stunned, looking up from her charts.

"Your smile. You're kind with patients and you mean it, but with other doctors you're cold and you hide yourself away. You hide your feelings. Why?"

She straightened her back and her blue eyes were wide with fear. "Patients are different. They're not in competition with me."

"You think residency is a competition?"

"Isn't it?"

"I never thought of it that way," he said.

"Surgery is a competition. Surgeons are competitive by nature."

"Well, I'm not here to compete. I'm here to learn and save lives."

Her expression had softened, but only for a moment, and then she'd turned back to charting.

That had been the first time she'd sort of let him in.

He learned after that she'd been raised by two tough-as-nails surgeons and she was good at locking away her emotions, but that smile—that was the smile that he fell for. It was almost as if she was letting him inside the walls she had put up to keep people out.

"Good." He pulled out his phone. "Give me the address and I'll meet you there in thirty minutes?"

"Sure." She took his phone and punched in the address of the Bridgers' training facility. "I'll see you in half an hour. I'll call George now and have him come down to the training center."

He nodded and took a step back, as if trying to distance himself.

He didn't really know what he was doing. Why was he going there?

Because she smiled. You're a sucker for that smile. Even after all these years.

Pearl smiled. She showed her softness toward a patient and she came to him and asked for help. That's when he melted for her, and here he was falling into the old trap again.

Once again Pearl had turned his whole world upside down.

"See you then."

The elevator opened, she got in and the door shut, and it was then he frowned. Angry at himself for letting her in again.

You're a softie, Calum.

And he hated himself for that.

He knew one thing—this was as far in as he was going to let her.

He wasn't making the same mistake twice.

CHAPTER TWO

CALUM FOUND THE Bridgers' training facility quite easily.

He knew where it was. His father had repeatedly invited him here since he won his medical award. Finding the place was the easiest part of this whole situation.

What am I doing?

He couldn't believe that he was actually here. He could have waited until this patient came to the hospital, but no, he had to offer to come here instead.

He had gotten carried away with memories when he saw Pearl. The way she cared for her patients got to him every time. If he hadn't been so reckless and chased after Pearl, he wouldn't have had to come.

You're doing this for the young athlete, not her. Remember that.

And that's what he had to focus on.

When he entered the modern building near

Haight-Ashbury, he was impressed by the new architecture that blended with the old. The Bridgers might be a fairly new team to the Bay area, but they were sparing no expense.

The last time he had talked to his father, he had gone on and on about the financials of the new team. Apparently it was okay to back a new professional sports team, and let his ex-wife and his children starve.

Of course, now his father saw some use in him since he won the scientific award and the large grant that went with it. Looking around at the reception area of the Bridgers' training center, Calum started to feel that old resentment in himself rising.

That old resentment he felt when his father would put work over family.

State-of-the-art equipment and a professionally decorated reception area with expensive art and marble floors—this is what his father valued over him.

Over his mother.

His father valued possessions.

He had to get control of himself; he wouldn't let his father in here. He wouldn't let his father interfere with his job. Calum had a cool, professional relationship with his father and that was it.

That's all it would be and he wouldn't let all those old emotions throw him into a tailspin. He had worn his heart on his sleeve once and had it shattered.

There was no way that he was going to do that again.

"Calum!"

He turned and saw Pearl walking toward him. His pulse quickened seeing her and he hated that she still had this effect on him.

He hated that he lost control.

"Pearl," he responded gruffly.

"I'm so glad you agreed to come here. George is having a hard day," she said gently.

"It's no problem."

"Good." There was some tension to that smile. Her back was ramrod-straight and she stood there smiling awkwardly.

Honestly, he felt the tension, too, and he kept his hands jammed in his pockets.

"Why don't you follow me?" Pearl suggested, turning.

"Okay." He fell into step beside her. He tried to keep his distance, but being so close to her

again, catching that whiff of her coconut sham-
poo, still felt the same as it did five years ago. It
was hard not fall into old patterns.

It was hard not to reach out and take her hand
like he used to.

So he walked rigidly beside her, trying not to
come in close contact.

"I know this is hard," she said, breaking the
silent tension.

"What's hard?" And he inwardly groaned, not
wanting to talk about it.

She turned to face him. "I don't want this to
be weird between us. You said you wanted to
be colleagues on this case and I want that, too."

"We are."

Pearl cocked one of her finely shaped brows.
"Come on, Calum. We're both adults, what happened—"

"We're not going to talk about what happened,"
he snapped, cutting her off. "That's in the past."

Her blue eyes widened, but only briefly.
"Okay."

"Let's focus on the patient," he said stiffly. The
last thing he wanted to do was talk about what
happened five years ago.

The last thing he wanted to do was feel any

kind of emotion that was attached to that horrible moment in his life.

Truth be told, the last thing he wanted to do was feel at all. And he was envious she seemed so detached from it all, but that's the way she had always been and why other residents, except Calum and a couple of others, had called her the ice queen.

Right now he wanted to think of her like that.

He didn't want to think about all the times the ice queen had melted under his touch and had set fire to his blood.

He was here to do work. That—focusing on the patient—was what he intended to do. Calum followed Pearl into an exam room. The young athlete, George Vaughn, was sitting on an examination table, his bad leg outstretched and with ice.

He smiled a bright smile, his dark eyes twinkling when he saw Pearl. Not that Calum could blame him—Pearl was a beautiful woman.

"Hi, Doc!"

"Hi, George, this is my colleague Dr. Calum Munro and he's one of the best orthopedic surgeons specializing in osteosarcoma."

George grinned at him and held out his hand.

Calum took his hand and shook it. The young man was strong, but wiry, which was good for a linebacker. He could run.

"It's a pleasure to meet you, Dr. Munro," George said politely.

"Same, George. How is your pain level today?" Calum asked, pulling over a rolling chair so that he could sit and examine the leg.

"It's about a seven. The ice is helping," George responded tightly.

Calum highly doubted the ice was helping. The lines in the young man's face told another story. The pain George felt was deep, bone pain. A tumor infiltrating the nerves. George was trying to put on a brave face, like most of the young men he had as patients tried to do.

He was glad George was determined to fight this cancer. You needed to remain strong to fight the disease, to beat it. You needed mental strength to keep going when your body wanted to give up.

Calum had seen it enough times. He had seen it in his mother.

"Do you mind if I have a look?" Calum asked.

"Go ahead." George winced as he leaned over and removed the ice pack. There was swelling near the knee and the moment he gently touched the area, George sucked in a deep breath.

Calum finished his examination, which included using his Doppler to listen to the blood flow in the leg.

"Do you think you can help me, Doc?" George asked hopefully.

"I'm going to look at your labs and your scans. From there I'll confer with Dr. Henderson about the best course of treatment." Calum couldn't give George an answer just yet. He didn't want to give false hope to the young man. Not until he had all the facts, but Calum was going to do his best to help him.

George smiled. "Thanks, Doc."

Calum grinned and patted the young man on the back.

"Let me help you," Pearl said, reaching out to grab George's arm as she and Calum helped him off the table. Pearl handed him his crutches. "Do you have a ride back to your place?"

George nodded. "Yeah, the coach brought me in and he's going to take me back. No doubt he wants to talk strategy."

"Strategy?" Calum asked.

Pearl laughed. "My friend George here, besides being one of the fastest linebackers I've seen in a while, is an excellent play strategist. He's been assisting the coach with that while he's on leave."

"Yeah, but that's not what I want to do for the rest of my life," George said quickly. "I want to be back on the turf."

"We'll do everything we can to make that happen," Calum said, instantly regretting his words.

Don't make promises you can't keep.

Only he couldn't help it. He felt bad that George was missing out. How would he feel if he couldn't live his dream of becoming a surgeon?

Life was not fair.

He was keenly aware of that from when they had lost the baby and then he had lost Pearl, too. Life had dealt him a raw hand and he was going to try and make sure that the same thing didn't happen to this young man. He couldn't guarantee success. It was cancer and there was no cure. Only treatments.

"Right," Pearl said cautiously.

"Dr. Henderson and I will strategize this afternoon," Calum teased, winking.

George grinned and opened the door. "Thanks, Docs!"

Pearl helped him out of the exam room and watched to make sure that he got down the hall, before she came back into the exam room and closed to the door. She crossed her arms, her lips pursed.

"So we're going to strategize, huh?" she asked.

"Of course. Isn't that what colleagues do?"

"Yes. That's what they do," Pearl answered, a bit stunned. She was pleased that Calum seemed so optimistic about George's cancer, because she didn't feel that way. Of course, Calum was always the more optimistic one.

Not that she could really blame him. With her upbringing and dealing with her parents, anyone could be more optimistic than her, but it still always amazed her Calum was more optimistic than her. His childhood had been no better. Still, over the years she was trying to improve herself. Trying to see that brighter side of life, but it was hard to do that with her parents always reminding her she wasn't good enough.

Everything good in her life had been taken from her. Everything.

"Stop crying, Pearl. You're embarrassing me!" her mother had hissed, shaking her as she stood

outside the hospital door where her grandmother had just died.

"But, Grandma... I can't... I miss her."

"You think you're the only one?" Her mother sighed, annoyed, and ran a hand through her hair frustrated. "Who will watch you now?"

Pearl wiped her tears. "I can stay with you. I won't cry. I promise. I won't cry."

Her mother sighed. "Crying shows weakness. You can't show weakness."

Pearl nodded. Inside she was bursting. Her heart was breaking. She wanted to cry, but if she did her mother would send her away. She swallowed the pain. It sat like a rock in her.

"I won't cry. I swear," she'd insisted.

Her grandmother had taken care of her, loved her, and then she had died.

Pearl always wanted that home back. She just didn't know how to get back there. To find something like that again.

And then she found Calum and got pregnant. She was terrified, but secretly she wanted a family. A real family. Maybe she could have and share that love she felt when she was a child and with her grandmother.

Then she had lost the baby. So it was hard to see the bright side, especially after that.

And even though it had been five years, it still stung.

It still felt as fresh as yesterday, but she swallowed that grief like she had when her grandmother died.

"So do you want to go somewhere and get a bite to eat?" he asked, pulling her out of her morose thoughts.

"What?"

"I haven't had lunch, it'll be a late lunch slash early dinner, but do you want to go out and maybe talk about how we're going to approach this case?"

She really shouldn't go out with him.

She should stay here and catch up on her work, but she didn't have a lot of work to do because the team was off today. Her team of capable physiotherapists and kinesiologists were with the athletes today. No one else was injured enough, which was great, but really her only patient was George.

And George had been seen to.

She could go out with him. They had to discuss George's file. It was work and nothing more.

Right.

And she was nervous. Her palms were sweaty as she rubbed her hands together.

"Sure." And she hoped her voice didn't shake It was just business. She had to keep telling herself that.

Calum had made it clear that they were just supposed to be colleagues. She should learn to keep her distance, but colleagues could have a meal together, couldn't they?

Maybe colleagues who didn't have a past like you have with Calum can just have a dinner together.

"Great. I do have some thoughts on George's case and I need your help on some of mine."

Pearl blinked a couple of times as she let that sink in. "Right, because I'm helping you with your caseload."

She was so nervous around him. She had to remind herself to keep calm, cool and collected.

They were here to work.

She had to stop thinking about the past.

"Exactly. We both win here and we're granting you privileges at the hospital, because I'm actually willing to take on George's case."

"And I appreciate that and I'm willing to help."

Pearl crossed her arms, hoping by doing so she could hold him off, or at least hold back her emotions, which were threatening to spill out.

He grinned. "So since you're on my service, I would like you to do some time in the hospital."

"You make that sound like a prison sentence." She smiled and relaxed a bit. "I agreed. Just tell me when you want me to be there."

Honestly, she was okay with this option and she was glad that he wasn't doing something foolish, like removing her from George's case. She was quite fine with working shifts at the hospital and assisting on some pro bono cases—because of her job she didn't get to do a lot of surgery. Her practice, with the team, was small and limited to sports injuries. It would be nice to get back into the operating room and do some of the surgeries she didn't often get to do.

Surgeries that had made her want to become an orthopedic surgeon.

The surgeries she excelled at when she was working with Dr. Chin.

There were times she questioned why she had left, but her focus had always been to work with a professional team. That was her goal.

Her grandmother had loved football and they

watched it every week. Any time there was a game on, her grandmother liked to take her to tailgate parties.

So working with a professional football team had always been her dream and when she lost the baby it seemed like the time to take the leap and make it happen.

And she didn't want to admit the real reason why she'd left San Francisco. She hadn't wanted to lose Calum. She had been afraid if she stayed things would become worse.

That he'd loathe her, like her parents loathed each other.

When they got together they had both had goals.

Goals that were both completely different, even if they were studying the same medical discipline.

Just like her parents. Her mother blamed her father for holding her back and vice versa.

She had never wanted that for her and Calum.

The thought of him loathing her was too much to even contemplate. So she had left.

Sure, he was cool with her, but they could work together. They were both professionals, both at the top of their fields. They hadn't lost that.

"When did you want me to report to you?" she asked tightly.

"Well, I won't be there, but show up for midnight. We get severe ortho traumas from local hospitals. Sometimes we get a bunch of cases, other nights we don't, but we're on call for them."

"Midnight is fine."

It had been a while since she did a midnight shift, but she'd weather it.

"I'm glad you're on board," Calum said. "So should we go have something to eat and talk business?"

Pearl smiled. "I'd like that."

And she would. That's all she wanted to talk about.

Business.

Not the baby. That was still too raw.

Pearl had to put away George's file and make sure her office was locked and that her staff knew where she was going. She liked the idea of grabbing something to eat with Calum, because she wanted to be able to work with him again.

She didn't want there to be any tension between the two of them while they handled George's case. Some of the best times of her life had been when they worked together.

He was smart, talented and so sure of himself, but not in an arrogant way.

It would be good being colleagues again. She'd missed that these last five years.

And truth be told, she missed him. Even though it was for the best and she had given him back his freedom, she had missed him.

She'd always missed him. Always wondered what he'd been doing, so she was looking forward to having this lunch with him and talking about cases, like they used to do.

Being with him had been a bright spot in her life. Having a late lunch and discussing a case would be like the good old days, when they had been friends and worked together.

Those were the days she missed.

And even though she didn't want to admit it, she was lonely.

Loneliness is for the weak, Pearl. Remember that.

Her father's voice droned on in her head. And she felt bad for feeling that emotion. That keen pang of loneliness.

Calum was waiting in the lobby and her heart

skipped a beat as she saw that he hadn't left, that it wasn't some sort of ruse, that maybe they could go back to being friends.

And that thought thrilled her. It made her happy.

It also scared her. She took a deep, calming breath before she approached him. She was so used to seeing him in just jeans, a T-shirt and beat-up old sneakers when he wasn't in his scrubs. The last five years and becoming chief of orthopedic surgery had changed him. He was still wearing jeans, but they weren't the same worn ones he always wore. These were pressed and new. They were well taken care of.

He was wearing a T-shirt, but a high-end one that complemented the relaxed sports jacket and there were no sneakers. Instead he wore nice dress shoes. He looked put-together and professional.

Calum took her breath away and she couldn't remember the last time that any man made her feel this way. Calum had been her first and, come to think of it, Calum had been her last.

She'd gone on other dates, but it was never the same.

No one else had made her swoon. Her pulse

began to race and she was suddenly so nervous again. She'd forgotten. Forgotten how he made her feel. How he got through all her defenses.

And she was annoyed at herself for still reacting this way.

Get a hold of yourself.

She had to remind herself that she was just here to work. Nothing more. She wasn't here to rehash their relationship.

Calum understood her and she understood him. It was over between them. It had been over for five years. She was here to work.

He smiled at her and there were a few more lines at the corners of his eyes, but he was wearing his late thirties quite well.

"Everything okay?" he asked.

"I just had to make sure my assistant knew where I was and that I'm not working with any player today and they're all with my team of physiotherapists. I shouldn't be paged, but I might be."

Calum nodded. "Well, the place I want to go to isn't far. In fact, you should remember the little Italian place near Buena Vista Park."

"It's still there?" Pearl asked, in amazement.

"Yes, Il Polpo Arrabbiato, and the wood-fired

pizza is still the same. It's a gorgeous day and I thought that was a nice quiet spot to go to strategize. And it's not a far walk."

"I would like that."

In fact, she liked that quite a bit. It had been one of their favorite haunts. It was cheap and cheerful.

"Here's to finishing residency!" She raised her glass of wine.

Calum smiled and clinked his glass with her. "Thank God!"

"And here's to the tackiest place in San Francisco," she teased.

"That, too." He took a sip of his wine, then set down the glass and took her hand.

A rush, a thrill at his touch, made her blush. He made her feel safe. She hadn't felt like this in a long time. She didn't pull her hand away. She moved closer and rested her head on his shoulder.

Savoring it.

Savoring the feeling of being held and cared for.

Pearl sighed. She'd forgotten about Il Polpo Arrabbiato.

They spent many a happy time there and going back seemed like they were going home.

Only she wasn't home. She didn't have a home or a family.

All she had was herself.

CHAPTER THREE

IT WAS AN ugly restaurant. Even after five years, it still was an ugly restaurant. Il Polpo Arrabbiato, also known as The Angry Octopus, was an Italian restaurant that was tucked in an old Victorian home that overlooked Buena Vista Park. It was painted a bright orange color and looked a bit out of place and not as stylish as the famous Painted Ladies or the Seven Sisters that were usually featured in San Francisco postcards.

It stood out like a sore thumb, but also seemed to fit in for the street.

Locals were used to the garish home. She hadn't been here in five years, but she'd forgotten how blindingly orange it was.

Even though it was an eyesore it was a wonderful restaurant and a great place to get a piece of wood-fired pizza in the Haight-Ashbury area. She couldn't even really remember how they discovered Il Polpo Arrabbiato.

And then it came back to her, like a sweet memory she hadn't been expecting.

"You'll like this place," Calum had insisted.

"I don't know. It's orange!"

"You said you wanted pizza," he stated firmly. *"This is the best in San Francisco."*

"How? I've lived here my whole life and I've never heard of or seen this place!"

"You grew up near the Presidio. This is my stomping ground."

She cocked an eyebrow. "You grew up in the Mission District. How is Haight your stomping ground?"

"Home sucked. I wandered the city a lot."

She nodded her understanding. Her home sucked, too. "It's an orange house, though, with an octopus on it. How does this serve the best pizza?"

"Trust me."

And she had.

She had a hard time trusting anyone. Her parents' constant broken promises to her left her wary of any kind of trust in anyone, but in that moment she trusted Calum for the first time.

Walking toward the restaurant, Pearl felt like she was stepping back in time.

The last time she'd been here was when they were celebrating the end of their medical boards, the last step to becoming surgeons. It was when they knew they were going to be surgeons. They were done school. It had been her, Calum and their friends Dianne and Jerome.

It had been a great night.

Too many carbs, lots of wine and laughter.

Pearl couldn't remember the last time she let loose like that.

After that night, things got a little crazy. She was pregnant, they were planning to get married and they were trying to plan their careers. They never went back, because there was no time.

It was a bit strange to be back here now. It was a bit surreal. She stopped just before crossing the street and tried to calm all the racing thoughts in her head. All the emotions she seemed to be losing control of. She took a deep breath, trying to slow her racing heart.

"You okay?" Calum asked. He stopped and looked back at her.

"It's been a while," she whispered, hoping that her voice didn't shake and that he didn't sense her emotion. Her cheeks flushed in embarrassment, for letting her control slip in front of him.

Her mother had always told her to never let anyone see your *weak* side. Surgeons needed to be confident and if she wasn't going to be a cardiothoracic surgeon like her parents wanted, then she had to exude confidence and maintain control. She hated that old tape of her mother that played in her head.

Although, Pearl didn't necessarily think it was weakness, but it had been so ingrained in her that she couldn't shake that humiliation that her mother always made her feel when she shed a tear.

"I know. When was the last time we were here?" he asked.

"After our boards," she laughed softly. "We drank a lot of wine that night."

Calum's eyes twinkled. "We did. It was the cheap stuff, too. I had such a hangover the next day."

"I remember," she replied dryly. "You know you can overcome a lot when you hear your significant other be sick, and so loudly."

Calum groaned. "Right. Well, I seem to recall not long after you suffered from morning sickness and it was rough."

She winced. It stung to think about it. She'd

thought she had a cold, but it was pregnancy. At first she didn't want any help, but Calum had been there, holding back her hair, bringing her cold cloths and water.

He had always been there. She was the one who left.

"I remember. We never did get back here after that night," she said, trying to change the subject back.

"No. I suppose we didn't," he said wistfully.

Her pulse quickened. She took a step back to center herself.

She shook her head, trying to shake away the remnants of those old times. They were in the past.

"You sure you're okay?" he asked again.

"I'm fine. I think I'm a little shocked that it hasn't changed at all."

"Well, they have a few more octopi decorations inside," Calum stated, grinning.

"So you come here often?" she asked, a bit hurt because she thought that this was *their* place and a really awful side to her couldn't help but wonder who else had been here with him.

Does it matter? You let him go.

Only, it did matter, even if she didn't want to admit it.

"Not that often, but sometimes." There was a hint of sadness in his voice, but only a hint and then it was gone. She understood. She was feeling the same way, but maybe, just maybe, they could have an enjoyable, productive lunch.

She wanted to work with him. Just like the good old days.

Even if things had changed.

"Come on."

She nodded and followed him. They crossed the street and walked inside, where she was blinded by the new octopi decorations. It wasn't just a few. It was like a kraken had come in, had a bunch of babies and left.

They were everywhere. It was tacky. It was trippy and it seemed completely in place for the Haight-Ashbury neighborhood.

"Goodness, it's like release the kraken or what in here," she muttered under breath.

He chuckled. "Is a kraken even an octopus?"

"I have no idea. It's a mythical creature with tentacles, I think." She smiled to herself. Even though this place was tacky and ugly, she'd forgotten how much she loved this quirky, offbeat place in San Francisco.

They found their old corner booth, but it had changed. It was outfitted with vinyl that resembled tentacles. Purple tentacles, but it was just something stitched into the vinyl and thankfully not real tentacles.

Calum chuckled and as they both slid in on the opposite sides of the booth.

"What?" she asked.

"You look horrified. Don't they have tacky places like this in New York?"

Pearl laughed. "I was trying to hide it."

"Hide what?" he asked.

"My horror," she said quietly.

"You're not doing a good job," Calum whispered.

She leaned over the table, which was painted to look like an eyeball. A big angry krakenesque eyeball staring up at her. It was creepy, but fun. "This place is tackier than I remember."

"It's why they're so popular with tourists. Where else can you have pizza that's themed with angry octopi?"

"I honestly don't know and I'm not sure that I want to find out," she chuckled.

Calum's eyes were twinkling. "Fair enough."

She opened the menu, glad to see a lot of familiar items still graced the pages, and she just hoped that the food hadn't changed that much, either. She was hoping that the pizza didn't have calamari on it or something.

"I know what you're thinking," he said, closing the menu.

"Do you?" she asked.

"You're wondering if the pizza comes shaped like the decor? No, it doesn't. They haven't gone that far. Yet. Don't put it past them, though— they add more octopi stuff all the time."

Pearl laughed. "Perhaps. Actually, I was more concerned that the pizza would come with bits and pieces of the decor."

"Oh, there's one like that. It's the seafood surprise, but the food is still the same."

Pearl wrinkled her nose. "Okay, noted. So, I don't get it."

"What?" Calum asked.

Pearl set down her menu and folded her hands across the menu. "You said that this restaurant hadn't changed."

"Well, there are bits that changed, but the pizza is still good. Even the seafood surprise."

"You've had that?"

Calum shrugged. "One night I was feeling a bit adventurous."

"And?" she asked, trying not to laugh.

"It was not a great experience."

Now, she couldn't help but laugh. It was so easy with Calum. He always knew how to get through her defenses. How to make her happy.

She'd forgotten and that scared her. She couldn't get hurt again. She couldn't let herself get carried away with Calum. It was better for both of them.

She knew she'd hurt him when she left, but it was for the best.

It was for the best.

Was it?

Right now, in this moment, she couldn't remember why she had thought it was best to leave. There were times over the last five years she had thought of coming back, but she had been afraid.

Her parents always made her feel bad about her mistakes and she was afraid of facing this mistake again.

She turned back to her menu, trying to rein in her emotions, her pain. Her heartache.

"You went quiet there," Calum remarked.

"Did I?" she asked, hoping that her voice didn't crack.

"You did."

"It's nothing."

"Pearl, it's clearly something."

She didn't want him digging through her walls. She didn't want to lose control of her emotions again.

"Maybe it is, but you told me you didn't want to discuss it."

"What's that?"

"The baby. Me leaving."

"No. I haven't forgotten and you're right. I don't want to talk about it," he sighed. "I can't."

And she understood. The last thing she wanted to do was make a scene. To lose control.

"Well, I better make a decision on what to eat so we can come up with a plan for George. I have to get back to the training facility soon." Inwardly she cringed. She wanted to talk with him like old times, but he wasn't ready and she wasn't sure she was, either. She was so upset at herself for allowing herself to fall right back into old habits. She thought that the time they spent apart would be enough to cure it all, but it wasn't.

Clearly it wasn't.

* * *

Calum didn't know what had come over Pearl, but one minute it was like the good old days again and then the next, she threw up her wall. And he wasn't comfortable talking about the baby. Not right now.

She hadn't been there for him. He had grieved alone and he wasn't going to talk about it now. She was right. They were here to talk about work and not reminisce about old times. He had to keep it professional with Pearl.

And maybe that was the best thing to do. Except it was so easy to laugh with her. He swore he would keep this professional, but he still cared for her.

If he wanted to keep it professional, he shouldn't have brought her here.

He was kicking himself now for suggesting it. This had been their place. He barely came here anymore. He had once or twice over the years because they did have good pizza and it was in close proximity to his house, but being here was hard.

And it wasn't the garish decor that made it hard.

This is where they came after brutally long shifts, where they vented about the day.

This is where their relationship went from being friends to something more.

He had come here when he wanted that connection with Pearl when she had gone for all those years. It seemed natural and right. They'd discussed so many cases here. It just seemed right to discuss another one.

He lost all sense of reasoning when it came to Pearl and he was just setting himself up for heartache, but there was another part of him, one that remembered how much better life was around her. How much he'd been in love with her. She made him feel like he wasn't alone anymore. Like he could have the family he always wanted.

The memories of their time together...

Those he couldn't shake, couldn't run away from. They were always there and it was that side of his brain that had driven his decision to bring her here.

"Have you chosen?" he asked, curious if she'd choose the same thing she always did.

Hawaiian. Which he found abhorrent because pineapple on a pizza was gross.

"The Hawaiian," she said, closing her menu.

He smiled and shook his head. "Typical."

"What?" she asked.

"Always the same," he teased.

"I'm not as adventurous as you having calamari on a pizza!"

"It wasn't just calamari."

She made a face, her nose wrinkling. "I don't want to know."

He laughed. "I've missed this."

Her expression softened. "I have, too."

Calum reached out to take her hand, but pulled back when the waitress came.

They both ordered, but when the waitress left, the conversation that only moments before had been so free and easy had come to a standstill.

Pearl could barely look at him. Why was this so hard?

They could be friends again. They could work together. They had worked well together. It didn't have to be anything but that, even if, deep down, he wanted it to be.

"I want to do targeted radiation first," Calum said, finally breaking the silence. They were here, after all, to talk about a plan for George. If she wanted to keep it business, then he would keep it that way, too.

It was probably for the best.

It kept him from wanting to talk about what happened all those years ago. It kept him from talking about the baby, about their loss. He didn't want to talk about it now or he'd lose control.

If this working relationship was going to succeed, he had to keep control of his emotions.

"That sounds like a good start."

"It is," he said. "That's why you've come to see me. My protocol has a high success rate."

"But it doesn't always work," she stated.

He pursed his lips together. "Why would you say that? You're so pessimistic sometimes."

Her eyes narrowed. "I'm a realist. You're far too optimistic."

"My optimism has saved lives. People suffering from cancer need all the hope they can get."

Pearl sighed. "Fine. You're right. It does. I know that, but what I want to know is what you'll do if your protocol doesn't work. You don't need to explain the process to me. I know your process and yes, it's why I came to you, but what will you do if it doesn't work?"

Calum swallowed a lump that had formed in his throat. He hated to discuss outcomes—every patient was so different and because of that every patient responded differently. It was a fine balance of medications, of treatments and the patient's DNA, which skewed the results. He didn't like to deal in absolutes, but sometimes, unfortunately there was no other choice.

"I would have to amputate."

Pearl's expression softened. "I hope we can avoid that. I would hate to see George's life ruined."

"I understand," Calum said gently. "But sometimes it's too far gone. Sometimes it doesn't work. If it worked all the time I would have the patent to the cure for cancer and I definitely don't have that, but I try to remain optimistic. I try all that I can before I have to opt to the alternative."

"Which is amputation?" she asked.

He nodded. "Yes. The only way to get rid of osteosarcoma, but I'm trying to be positive that this protocol will work on George. There are many factors that might not make it successful."

"I understand."

"I knew you would. You're a brilliant doctor, Pearl. You did the right thing coming to me and asking for my help."

She smiled, and the hardness in her eyes, the indifference that tainted her expression when she pulled away from him, melted. She let down that wall she always seemed to throw up to keep people out.

This was the Pearl he remembered.

"Well, I hope that it doesn't come to that. I hope your protocol works."

Calum nodded. "So do I. I hope we caught it early enough. Did he say when the symptoms started?"

"Just before he was drafted by the Bridgers. His mother couldn't afford to send him to a good doctor at the time. It was all she could do to take care of his siblings and he was off in college. He was also on a scholarship, so if he did feel anything, he was ignoring it. He had to play in order to stay in college."

Calum scrubbed his hand over his face. "So he could've been ignoring the early symptoms for quite some time then?"

Pearl shrugged. "Maybe, but I'm choosing to believe him. Although, he didn't come to me with the issues. It was an injury and that's how I found it."

Why were people so stubborn?

It was a cruel twist of fate that George probably had the symptoms for some time and was too scared to do anything about it. His own mother had done the same. She had spent all she had on him and his sister, Sharon. She had been afraid of going to the doctor to find out what she had. She had worried it would cost too much.

She had ignored her symptoms so long it had been too late when she finally did see someone.

George's leg hadn't broken yet, so Calum was hopeful that they caught it early, but he wasn't sure.

"So you were going to tell me about my other duties?" Pearl asked.

"Your other duties?"

She frowned at him. "You said because you're the chief of orthopedic surgery and because I was given special privileges and you were doing this work for the Bridgers that I now work for you. I'm helping you ease your caseload."

He grinned. "That's right. I momentarily forgot about that."

"Well, that's not surprising. Bad seafood, especially bad seafood on a pizza, can really mess with your head." She was teasing him and he couldn't help but smile.

Remember why you're here. Remember what happened last time.

Only, it was hard because of the pain she caused him when she was sitting so close to him, in one of their favorite places, and teasing him like she did five years ago.

His pulse thundered between his ears. She was so close. All he wanted to do was reach out and touch her, to pull her in his arms and kiss her.

After five years, he still wanted her, and he was annoyed that being this close to her affected him like this. So he tried to focus on her leaving.

It was difficult to remember the pain, because he didn't want to.

Because the pain was too much to bear. And he'd had enough pain to last a lifetime. All he wanted was just a bit more of the happiest time of his life. All he wanted was Pearl.

They ate their pizza and talked about George and the other surgeries that Calum had planned. There was a particular spinal surgery that he wanted her help with. She always had a knack for nerves and the regular surgeon he worked with wasn't going to be in town when the patient wanted the surgery done.

They walked back to her training facility so that he could collect his car and go home.

It was awkward walking the streets back to her office. He wanted to take her hand like he always used to, but he couldn't. So he jammed his hands in his pockets again.

"Thanks for the lunch," she said quietly.

"Thank you for helping out tonight."

"Of course. I'm looking forward to it." She smiled and then looked away, her cheeks flushed.

He didn't know what else to say to her and since their lunch was late, the streets were busy with people heading for home. It was rush hour. Thankfully, he didn't live far from the hospital, so it wouldn't take him long to get home to his dog Max, who was probably eagerly awaiting his return so they could head down to Golden Gate Park and have a walk.

"Have you found a place to stay yet?" he asked.

"Yes. I have a small house not too far from here. The team rented it for me. It's a pretty modern house. Not as stylish as the Seven Sisters, but it's nice and an easy walking distance from the training center. I don't have a car yet." She looked like she wanted to ask him if he was still living in the same place, their old apartment, but he wasn't.

When she had left, it had been too much to bear being there alone without her and without the baby. He much preferred his new house, which happened to be just around the corner from the Seven Sisters.

"I don't live in our old place," he said quickly.

A blush tinged her cheeks and she looked embarrassed. "No, I didn't suppose that you would. That was a very small place in the Mission District."

"Right. I actually own a house, just around the corner from the Painted Ladies. It's a small house and definitely not brightly painted, but Max and I like going to Alamo Square Park."

"Max?" she asked.

"He's my dog. He's a mutt. A rescue. I think he's part sheepdog, because he's black and white, but there's something else in him because he's a big fella." Calum couldn't help but smile thinking about Max.

"I wish I had time for a dog, but I'm always on the move."

"Yes. Well, it's hard to put down roots when you're always running."

Her expression hardened and he knew then that he'd stepped too far.

"Well, I don't really have experience with roots," Pearl said stiffly.

"No. I suppose you don't."

He wasn't sure how they were going to be able to work together when he kept putting his foot in his mouth and then he realized they had made it back to the training facility.

"Well, thank you for the late lunch and again, thank you for taking on George. I should have his lab work to you in a day or so, and let me know when his scans are scheduled."

"I will. And I plan to see you tomorrow around eleven for that surgery I mentioned. The spinal surgery."

"Of course, and I'll be on call tonight. Have a good evening, Calum." She turned her back on him and walked back into the Bridgers' training facility. He just stood there, watching her walk away.

Why did he think that he could do this?

Why did he think that he could work with Pearl again?

He should've said no. He could've asked another surgeon to help with his other cases.

He should've turned her away, but when it came to her, even after five years he was a push-over.

And he was going to pay for his soft heart, and he wasn't sure he could deal with more pain.

CHAPTER FOUR

COFFEE IS GOOD.

She was tired. It had been a long time since she had done an overnight shift and now that she thought of it, it hadn't been since residency days.

She'd done long surgeries—surgeries that had to be done after a game. She'd been on the sidelines when players were taken off the field, but it had been a long time since she sat in an emergency room waiting for orthopedic injuries because the hospital was only sent severe cases. It was quiet tonight, which made the time drag on and on.

There had been some post-op patients that had been filtered through, but that was about it. Though she wouldn't comment on the quiet activity. That was a jinx waiting to happen.

"Look alive, Henderson!"

Pearl sat up and relaxed when she saw it was Calum in his scrubs. He was grinning and his eyes were twinkling mischievously.

"I thought you were off tonight?" she remarked.

"I was, but I felt bad. Your first night back and I left you on your own."

"I've done this before, you know," she teased. "But I appreciate you checking up on me."

"Solidarity and all that." He leaned over the desk. "The spinal fusion is booked for eleven. No point in going home since your done at four. You remember where the on-call rooms are?"

Warmth crept up her cheeks. She remembered vividly where they were and what happened in one. She remembered one particularly heated stolen moment. His hands on her skin.

His kisses, his caresses, the pleasure.

And just recalling the way it felt to be in his arms made her blood heat. It didn't help he was standing so close to her, wearing the same color scrubs he wore that night.

Don't think about it.

She cleared her throat, trying to break the nervous tension. "Yes. And I'll be ready for the spinal fusion. I'm looking forward to it."

"Good."

The phone rang at the desk and Calum leaned over to answer the call. His arm brushed hers and a tingle of electricity went through her. Just that simple touch made her body zing with need.

"Right. We'll be ready. How far out? Okay." He hung up the phone.

"What's up?"

"Accident. Severe crush injuries. A transport rolled over on a pickup truck."

Her eyes widened. "And the truck driver is the one with the crush injuries?"

Calum nodded. "It's his right side. Bones crushed, possible nerve damage. You think you're up for the challenge?"

"Yeah. How far out?"

"Ten minutes."

She stood. "Let's go."

Pearl followed Calum to the ambulance bay, where he helped her into a trauma gown and gloves. Her adrenaline was pumping. It had been a while since she was here, in this situation.

And a really long time since she'd worked with Calum.

The siren grew louder as the ambulance came closer, until it was in their bay and the doors of the rig opened.

"Massive trauma from that pileup. San Francisco General thinks this guy would be better off here with you, Dr. Munro," the paramedic said.

Calum nodded. "Anyone else they need to send, we'll take them."

The paramedic nodded and Pearl helped as they unloaded the patient. Pearl could see the damage to the right side of the patient's body, even just from a quick glance.

And the way the man's hand was, she wasn't sure how much could they save.

"Vitals are good," Calum said.

"CT scan was done at San Francisco General. No serious injuries to the vital organs," the paramedic said. "Kind of amazing."

"Yeah, for sure." Pearl helped push the gurney in.

"We need to get him up to the OR floor," Calum said. "Dr. Henderson, can you go over the file with the paramedic and meet me on the operating-room floor?"

Pearl nodded. "Of course."

Calum motioned to a couple of residents as they took away the trauma patient. He used to complain to her of being a control freak, but he was *just* as addicted to work as she was. He told her that work kept his mind off of things and he always kept busy.

She understood and respected that.

She worked to be the best, to please her parents, which over time she learned not to care too much about.

"Here's his file, doctor," the paramedic said. "All the information from San Francisco General."

"Thanks."

The paramedic nodded and returned to his rig.

Pearl glanced at the images. So much damage, yet his spine was intact and his major organs unharmed. She closed the file. It was going to be a long night, but it was these kind of challenges that had driven her to orthopedic surgery, much to her parents' disappointment. Neither of them felt like she should do this specialty.

Of course, she'd never been able to please them. Right now, none of that mattered.

But tonight she'd save a life. Tonight she'd do the best she could and give this patient a chance.

It had been a grueling surgery and Calum needed a few hours of sleep before his scheduled spinal decompression. He wouldn't have been able to handle that trauma without Pearl at his side.

There had been so much damage and Pearl had been right there beside him, working with him, and he didn't have to explain anything to her, like he did to the residents. He'd forgotten what it was like to work with her.

When they worked together she always knew the next move. She was a talented surgeon and he wanted this kind of talent on his staff.

They were able to save the man's arm and hand. The patient's hip needed to be replaced, but the pelvis was cracked and needed time to heal.

There would be more surgeries on their trauma patient, named John, but not tonight.

John's body had been through enough.

He stifled a yawn and closed the door quietly to the darkened on-call room. He knew Pearl was in here and he didn't want to wake her.

"You don't need to creep. I'm awake," she said in the darkness.

"Why aren't you asleep? You sound tired."

"I was wondering how John was."

"Stable. Vitals are good."

"Good." She yawned—he heard it and yawned, too.

"Don't. Yawns are contagious," he teased.

She chuckled softly. "I know. Sorry. I can't help it."

He sat on the bed across from hers. In the dim light coming through the blinds, he could sort of see her.

Barely, though.

He knew she was sitting cross-legged, her back to the wall.

And it was like that night five years ago when they locked the door and made love for the first time. His blood heated thinking of that night, of being with her.

"The beds are still uncomfortable," she remarked. "Have they changed at all since I left?"

"I doubt it."

"You should do something about that."

"I'm head of orthopedics, not chief of surgery."

"Not yet. Wasn't that your goal?" she asked.

"One day." It had been his goal to prove to his father he was a hard worker. That he deserved more than his father gave him. Except in five years, he realized it didn't matter. His father only doled out attention when it suited him.

Calum was tired of chasing after him.

After Pearl.

His stomach twisted in a knot.

"I'm going to try and get some sleep. Good work tonight, Pearl. It was good to work with you again."

"Same, Calum. Same."

Calum lay there in the dark listening to her breathing, until it went from light to deep, when he was sure she was asleep.

He rolled over on his back, still listening to her, and closed his eyes.

All he could see was that moment after they had made love. The two of them curled up on the small bed, their bodies pressed tight together, his arms around her as he listened to her sleep.

It didn't feel right to be so far away and it took every ounce of strength not to get up and go to her.

To hold her.

I've got to get out of here.

Calum got up and tiptoed to the door. He paused and watched her for a moment while she slept. He kneeled down beside her and lightly touched her face.

Her skin was so soft. Just like he remembered.

Leave now.

He left the on-call room He'd sleep in his office. He had to put some distance between him-

self and Pearl before he lost all sense of reason
and curled up next to her.

Pearl woke up and expected to find Calum there,
but he wasn't. She knew he'd left because the
moment she mentioned his old desire to become
chief of surgery it grew awkward. He tensed up.
She knew that they were both circling around the
issue. How they both still cared for each other.
She thought their years apart were enough time
to get over him. They weren't.

He'd remembered that night in the on-call
room, too, and she was glad she was so exhausted that she was able to fall asleep fast.

Maybe she should've tried to find another surgeon for George, but George was such a good
kid and he deserved the best chance for recovery, and his best chance just happened to be Dr.
Calum Munro.

Working with him on that trauma case just re-
affirmed that coming to Calum was the best decision she could have made for George.

Pearl slept, but she felt like she spent the whole
time in the on-call room tossing and turning.
She couldn't get Calum out of her head. How
good it was to work together on John and how

every inch of this hospital reminded her of her heartache and her loss, but also the best times of her life.

She missed it here.

She missed those times, her friends, the companionship, the job.

The baby.

Calum.

She couldn't stop thinking about how easy it was with him. How quickly they fell back into old habits and teasing, but she also remembered the times they argued. When they'd disagree during their residency.

When they worked together it ran hot and cold. Pearl knew first-hand what that was like. She had grown up with two parents who were constantly at each other's throats. One minute they were toe-to-toe screaming at each other and the next minute they were locked in a passionate embrace.

Of course, they were also having lots of passionate embraces with other people outside of their marriage vows.

At least she'd never done that, but Pearl didn't want passion. Not like that.

That toxic volatile passion her parents had. It

made her ashamed so she never talked about it. No one really asked, anyway. She said she came from a broken home and that was enough explanation.

Her parents' ridiculous marriage didn't need to be broadcast.

She wanted something else. Passion yes, but camaraderie, friendship. She wanted what she had with Calum, but she'd ruined that.

She groaned inwardly, frustrated that all she could suddenly think about was the first time they kissed, because that first time they kissed had lit some kind of spark inside her, one that had never been lit before.

And then that kiss led to a lot more.

And then, eventually, heartache, but she couldn't get Calum out of her head. And after being with him today, joking with him and talking with him, it was just so easy to fall back into those old routines.

Which she didn't want, but also she really did. Deep down.

So now, because of her restless night, she was walking into the attending lounge, tired and hoping that there was still that awful, black, strong coffee there. Dr. Chin used to refer to it as motor oil and she could use a couple of cups of that before she went into surgery with Calum. Especially before she went into a surgery that was going to take hours, which meant hours and hours of working with Calum.

Even though she was tired and worried about seeing Calum again, part of her was actually excited about the thought of performing surgery with him. That was another thing they were good at. They were good in the operating room together and she hoped that they would be again.

When she got to the doctors' lounge she was thrilled to see that Dr. Chin's motor oil was still there. She smiled and pulled a mug out of the cupboard, ready to pour herself a big coffee.

"Calum told me you were back, but I didn't quite believe it!"

Pearl turned around and smiled when she saw a familiar face standing in the doorway.

"Dianne! I didn't know you were still here! I thought you and Jerome bought a ranch outside of the city!"

Pearl was surprised to see her old friend, Dr. Dianne Lopez. She was another resident who had come up with her and Calum but worked with anesthesia. She had married Jerome before Pearl left, and the last she'd heard they had bought a ranch just outside of Sonora, California.

She gave Dianne a big hug. She was overcome with emotion. Her heart swelled and it was all she could do to contain the emotions overcoming her.

Dianne had been her first *real* girlfriend.

And though they kept in touch it was never the same as getting a hug in person. And she hadn't seen Dianne or Dianne's son Derek in a long time. Not since Derek was a little baby.

Dianne stepped back and smiled. "It's so good to see you. You haven't changed a bit in five years."

Pearl snorted. "I find that hard to believe."

Dianne laughed. "You look good."

"So do you. How is Derek?"

"Good," Dianne said, sitting down. "We're almost finished our full transition from San Francisco to Sonora. Jerome has a practice out there. He switched specialties from being an anesthesiologist and is a family doctor."

"Wow, good for him. How long of a commute is it from your place to here?" Pearl asked as she sat next to her on the couch.

"It's two and a half hours on a good day. This

is actually my last couple of days work here at this hospital and then I'm transferring to one in Sonora."

"So the move is almost permanent then?" Pearl asked, disappointed, but she knew that it had always been Dianne and Jerome's dream to own a big piece of land out in the country and raise kids. They had made it work.

And Pearl was a bit envious of that. Even though she tried to tell herself she had never wanted a family, even though her mother told her being tied down with a family ruined her career and even though Pearl was afraid it would never work out, she still wanted that.

What she would never have.

"My last day is tomorrow. I am taking some time off before I start my new position. I start that in the New Year."

"It sounds wonderful. I'm so happy for you. Sad that I move back to San Francisco and you're leaving."

Dianne smiled sadly. "I know, but you know this is what Jerome and I always wanted and we were finally able to make it happen."

"At least I get to work with you for a few more days." Pearl finished the coffee and winced.

"Yeah, it's still pretty bad. I can't believe that you and Calum drink that crap."

"Drink what?"

Pearl tried not to choke on her coffee when Calum walked in. Her heart skipped a beat when she saw him and she hoped that she wasn't blushing. He'd occupied her mind all night and she hadn't had enough coffee yet to deal with seeing him.

"That motor oil that Dr. Chin drank." Dianne shook her head. "It was awful."

Calum chuckled and poured himself a mug. He glanced at Pearl briefly, but just briefly, like she was an afterthought.

"It's fuel," he responded.

"Yeah, and I bet it could fuel a car!" Dianne stood up. "Well, I'm going to ready the patient for the surgery."

Calum nodded. "Okay. We'll be down soon. I want to catch Pearl up on the surgery."

Dianne nodded and then gave her another quick hug, which calmed her nerves. "It's so good to see you again."

"Same." Pearl hoped that her voice didn't crack and betray her nerves, but she was glad that Dianne was going to be in the operating room.

She didn't have too many friends from her residency days, but Dianne and Jerome were always friendly faces.

So was Calum's.

She shook away that thought and tried to finish the coffee, but Dianne was right—it was so bitter, so awful. She was used to drinking nicer stuff in New York. Lattes and cappuccinos. Stuff with artisanal foam, not stuff that was bubbling long after it was boiling.

"I'm glad to see you haven't given up the old tradition of having coffee before a surgery," Calum said offhandedly.

"If you can call this coffee." Pearl winced again and set down the mug. "I was actually looking forward to it when I first came in here. I think I remembered it fondly with nostalgia and now..."

"Yes?" he asked.

"Yeah, nostalgia and fond memories have betrayed me."

"First the uncomfortable beds and now the coffee. New York has made you soft." He was teasing her.

"You look tired."

He had dark circles under his eyes, but he still looked good.

He nodded. "Didn't sleep well last night."

"I did." *Eventually.*

He chuckled. "I'm glad you're able to help me today. Especially after last night."

"A promise is a promise. So where did you sleep?" she asked.

His eyes widened—she'd caught him off guard. "I thought you were asleep?"

"I'm a light sleeper."

"Since when?" he asked.

"For a year or so. Also, those mattresses suck. So where did you sleep?"

He chuckled. "Which is why I slept on the couch in my office."

"Lucky."

"Not really. The couch fits two people, sitting upright. It's not long enough to lie flat. Hence the coffee."

"Great. Since when did we get too old for all-nighters?" she teased.

"I don't know. And I'm not old."

"I feel old this morning," she groused, trying to stretch.

"Hardly."

Warmth flood her cheeks and her stomach did

a flip in anticipation. She cleared her throat. "So today's surgery?"

He nodded. "So today's surgery is a spinal decompression, but on a patient with achondroplasia and I remember that was one of your first solo surgeries."

Pearl smiled, secretly pleased he remembered. "That's right. I haven't done a spinal decompression in some time. Usually, my surgeries involve torn ligaments in the knee or shoulder. Anything to do with running or throwing."

"Well, this patient has had hip replacements done and knees done, but he's an actor and he slipped and fell during a stage performance. He didn't break his back, but something snapped and a disc in his cervical spine became impinged. Because of his achondroplasia the space was already narrow and now it's threatening to impinge the spinal cord. I'm hoping to do a decompression and not have to fuse the spine, but I may have to. I won't know until we get in there."

"You realize that he's going to have issues with airways and bleeding?"

Calum nodded. "Yes, and that's why I insisted that Dianne was our anesthesiologist. She's the best and she's done multiple surgeries on achondroplasia and skeletal dysplasia patients. They are difficult to get an airway and to maintain an airway. I want the best working on him, which is why I'm glad you're here. He's one of my top patients."

Warmth flooded her cheeks at his compliment. "I'm glad that I can help."

It felt nice he was complimenting her. It felt good to be appreciated by a fellow surgeon. Especially one she respected.

One she cared about.

Calum chugged back the rest of his coffee. "Well, we better get down there. I'll show you where you can get some fresh surgical scrubs."

Pearl nodded. "Thank you."

She wouldn't mind changing out of the disheveled scrubs.

"Do you remember where the surgical floor is or do I have to walk you down there?" Calum teased as he stood up to leave. "Last night was a blur."

"I think I can find my way down to the surgical floor. I will be there in ten minutes."

Calum nodded and made his way to the door, only to turn back. "I scheduled George to have scans this evening. I'm hoping that we'll be done the surgery by then, but spinal decompressions can take a while."

"I don't need to be there while George has a scan. His mother is in town now and he has his coach. I would like to see the scans as soon as they're done, though."

Calum nodded. "I'll let our radiologist know. I'll see you down there."

Pearl breathed a sigh of relief when Calum left. She found her locker and inside was a set of scrubs. She quickly changed out of the scrubs she slept in into the familiar colored scrubs that she remembered wearing when she worked here.

"Hey," Dianne said, coming back into the doctor's lounge.

Pearl was surprised. "Hey, I thought you were with the patient?"

"He had some more questions for Calum before he would let me even put an intravenous in, so I thought I would come back here and ask you a question."

Pearl braced herself for a personal question. Dianne knew that she and Calum had planned to get married before Pearl had lost the baby. She was hoping that Dianne wouldn't try to dig any further.

Dianne had been pregnant with her first the same time that Pearl had been pregnant, and Derek was the same age her child would have been.

It was why she only kept in touch with Dianne through emails. It was sometimes hard to know Dianne and Jerome were so happy with their son while also knowing that if she hadn't lost her child, she would be a mother to a five-year-old, too.

"What do you need to know?" Pearl asked hesitantly.

"What're you doing next weekend?"

"Next weekend?" Pearl asked, confused.

"Are you going to see your parents?"

A ball of dread formed in the pit of her stomach. Her parents would want to see her, since she moved back, but she didn't want to see them. She hadn't seen them in two years and that was fine by her.

"No. I won't be going to see them. I'll be here in San Francisco. Maybe I'll catch up on some work."

"You don't have to be on call for the Bridgers?" Dianne asked.

"No," Pearl said, confused. "They're not playing that weekend. What are you trying to get at, Dianne?"

"Since I haven't seen you in forever and you're back in the area I want you to come out to the ranch next weekend. Jerome wants to show off his new practice to you."

Pearl smiled. It was a nice offer, but she wasn't sure that she wanted to spend next weekend with a happy family. Then again, she really didn't want to be alone.

"It's an awesome offer, can I think about it?"

Dianne nodded. "Of course. I know I'm springing it on you, but when I texted Jerome that you were here and I had seen you…he got so excited. The four of us used to be inseparable."

A lump formed in her throat. "I know. I'll think about it."

Dianne smiled. "Good. I'll see you down there."

Dianne left and Pearl leaned against the open door of her locker. She would love to go and spend time with Dianne and Jerome, but it was Dianne's comment about how the four of them had been inseparable.

It was true.

They'd spent a lot of time together as two couples when she and Dianne had been pregnant together.

It was sort of like a dream. That moment in her life when she was happy and she almost had it all.

One that she had never expected and one that she still mourned the loss of.

She couldn't go to Dianne and Jerome's ranch.

Why not?

The other alternative was to spend her weekend off alone. She had no desire to visit her parents. Her mother was in Los Angeles and her father was in Seattle. She could fly to one of their places. Each of them had begged her to come and see them more often, but Pearl had a hard time facing them and the toxicity both of them spewed.

Their relationship was the reason why Pearl really didn't believe in happily-ever-afters. She tried to believe in forever and happiness, but that had turned out so painful.

Of course, there were exceptions, like Dianne and Jerome, who honestly seemed to be happy and had been together for a long time. Now they were living out the dream they always talked about.

It hit her hard that she really didn't have any dreams.

She didn't know what she wanted out of life, other than being a surgeon, which she had become.

She sighed and shook her head, trying to dispel her disappointment, her grief. There was no place for those thoughts here today. Today she had to be that surgeon that she had become. That was the only good thing in her life.

She was a surgeon and she knew how to save a life.

Just not her own, apparently.

Pearl glanced up a couple of times to see Calum standing on the opposite side of the operating table. Their patient was in the prone position to access the spine.

It was always tricky with a patient who had skeletal dysplasia because it was difficult to get a proper airway, but Dianne was good at her job.

It was good to be in the operating room again and working on something that was not a sports injury.

Well, not technically a sports injury. The patient was an actor and had insisted on doing his own stunts, which was why they were trying to decompress the spine. She assisted Calum in the delicate surgery, but he was the lead surgeon.

And it had been far too long since she'd worked with him on a surgery. She had forgotten what a talented surgeon he was and it just reinforced her decision to have him work with George.

Calum was George's best chance.

As if sensing she was watching him, he briefly glanced up. His eyes crinkled at the corners and she knew he was smiling behind the mask.

"How does it feel to be doing a decompression again, Dr. Henderson?" he asked from behind his mask.

"It's great to be back." And it was, she just forgot herself there for a moment. "It's a pleasure to be working with you again, Dr. Munro. I had forgotten what a talented surgeon you were."

And it was the truth. Coming back here and working with Calum was like coming home.

His blue eyes crinkled again and she hoped that was a smile and not a grimace behind his surgical mask.

"Ditto," he responded.

"Ditto?" she teased.

He chuckled as he continued to work. "Yes. Ditto."

Pearl smiled to herself. "Your compliments embarrass me, Dr. Munro." She did enjoy his compliments, but she also forgot how fun it was to banter with him back and forth across the table.

He cocked an eyebrow. "You haven't changed a bit. Can we focus?"

"I am focusing," she responded. "Or have you forgotten that I do idle chitchat during surgery. Especially when I think that surgery is going smoothly."

"I did forget," he responded dryly.

There were a few small laughs from the nurses and interns who were observing the surgery. Even Dianne was laughing a bit.

"I take it then you haven't changed and you still want almost absolute silence while you're working."

"I prefer that. Yes," Calum said. "Of course, being taught by Dr. Chin, I learned to work in noise."

Pearl smiled again. Dr. Chin had the propensity to blast music—in particular, Queen—especially when he was doing delicate procedures. It was when the patient wasn't doing well that the operating room fell silent, so the silence in Calum's room was making her a bit uncomfortable.

"So why don't we put some music on in here? The patient is responding well," she said.

"Do you blast music?" Calum asked.

"In fact, I do. I guess I adopted Dr. Chin's style."

Calum chuckled again. "I never really thought of a surgical playlist before."

"I've read studies that if music is playing it actually can help with blood pressure."

Calum cocked an eyebrow and looked at her in disbelief. "What?"

"I'll forward you that report." Pearl suctioned where some blood was pooling and it was then she saw that this was no longer a simple spinal decompression.

"Dammit," Calum muttered. "Do you see that?"

"Yes, it's wearing away at the spinal cord. There's no room for the decompression to go."

"I'm going to have to fuse him." Calum began to pull out the instruments and moved quickly to change his plan. "The patient didn't want a fusion, because a spinal fusion is going to take more time to heal and there will be more physiotherapy for him. He was pretty specific about not wanting a fusion because of his work."

"There's no choice in this case. Unless he wants to be a paralyzed."

Calum nodded. "Yep. No choice."

They both worked quickly, turning the spinal decompression surgery. And Pearl was glad to work with Calum. They had been trained by the same brilliant surgeon and even though they hadn't done a surgery together in five years, it was like they'd never been apart. There were no questions, there was no confusion. They worked together seamlessly.

It was like they were one.

And it felt right.

The surgery took longer than Calum planned. He knew that Pearl wanted to be there for George when he had his scan. In fact, there was a call into the operating room as they were working on the fusion. Pearl had been pulled away and he thought that she was going to walk away from their surgery for her high-paying VIP patient.

Really, she had no investment in staying and

he could handle a spinal fusion on his own, but Pearl returned.

She told him that she'd explained to George's coach why she couldn't be there and George had no problem with her not accompanying him to the MRI. He'd had MRIs before. So when the surgery was finished, Pearl left before they closed up his patient, so that she could check the scans and Calum had no problem with that.

He was impressed and glad that her priorities still seemed to be the same. Saving lives.

He thought when she left for that job out east with that first sports team, that he'd been wrong about her from the beginning. He'd thought the most important thing to was her job. Pearl had always talked about her parents putting career and the almighty dollar before family. Just like his father.

He was hurt and disappointed that she ran off and did that, but perhaps he'd been wrong about. She didn't go running off to babysit George. She'd stayed and done the surgery with him and she'd been a tremendous help to him. Maybe he was wrong about her and that thought upset him, because then he was the fool for letting her go.

Calum had forgotten what it was like to work with her.

It was like coming home.

Don't think like that.

He shook away that thought.

He couldn't let himself associate Pearl with home. Not that he really knew what home was. He'd thought he'd found that once, and when she left he hadn't really associated anything with home since. Other than his dog, Max.

After the patient was taken to the intensive-care unit and he updated the family, Calum made his way down to radiology to see if Pearl was still there and he saw that she was.

She was sitting in a darkened room, in front of a computer, hunched over, and she appeared stressed. She was frowning and worrying her bottom lip and he knew that expression well. It was the same expression when she broke the news that she was pregnant to him, but it wasn't the same expression when she told him she'd lost the baby.

That expression had been without emotion. It was flat, cold and detached. Like she was lost. Only he'd been lost, too, in that moment, but he felt like he didn't have the right to feel so lost.

He hadn't been the one carrying the baby, but he still grieved their loss just the same. Even when he thought about her like that, he wanted to hold her in his arms and comfort her, but he was sure that she would push him away just like she'd done all those years ago.

"Thanks for your help," he said gently from the doorway.

She tore her eyes from the computer screen and seemed momentarily surprised to see him standing there.

"What?"

"Your help with the patient and the spinal fusion."

She relaxed. "Right. No problem. It was good working with you again."

"Why are you still here? You should go home and rest."

"Can't. Stuff came up," she said, not looking at him.

"You seemed entranced by the computer. Is it George's scans?" he asked.

She nodded and he pulled up a chair beside her so that he could see the scans. The moment he saw them, a coil of dread unfurled in his belly.

It was the most extensive osteosarcoma he'd

seen. And compared to the last scans done, not that long ago, it had grown. And now he was having a bad feeling that he might not be able to save the leg.

That he might fail at this and let down Pearl and George. His father had let down his mother and Calum didn't want to let down Pearl.

He didn't want to be like his father.

Aren't you? You're so focused on work.

He shook away that thought and studied the images.

"It's extensive," he said quietly.

"It's bad. I've never seen one grow this fast," Pearl whispered. "It's…awful."

"And what would you tell him?" Calum asked seriously.

"What do you mean what would I tell him?"

"If you were the surgeon?"

Pearl sighed and scrubbed a hand over her face. "I would say that amputation is the only course of treatment. If it were me, but I haven't worked on enough osteosarcomas. I haven't developed a plan, an award winning aggressive treatment of osteosarcoma like you have."

"Pearl, don't pin all your hopes on me." And

he was serious. This cancer was dangerous, it was the most aggressive he'd seen in a long time.

The last time he had seen something like this was just after Pearl left, when he worked as much as he could with Dr. Chin. Work kept him busy and kept his mind off the loss of both Pearl and the baby.

It was on a teenage boy.

The osteosarcoma had been just like this. Calum had been full of hope that they could save the leg, but by the end there was no way he could. After multiple surgeries and lots of pain for the young man, they still had had to amputate.

It was then that Dr. Chin told him that sometimes the best help they could give someone, especially with a terminal diagnosis, was to do no harm.

Calum didn't want to accept that, but over the years, he has learned that Dr. Chin was right and sometimes there was nothing to be done.

Only, it was that sense of helplessness that drove him to work on his treatment plan for situations like this. And that boy might have lost his limb, but he was still alive and cancer-free.

Pearl then reached out and took his hand. It

surprised him and he couldn't push away her hand, because he liked the reassurance she was giving him.

It felt good.

It felt so right.

"I have faith in you, Calum. I think you can do this."

"You're wrong." Her eyes widened and he squeezed her hand. "We can do this together."

And he couldn't believe that he was saying that.

Pearl nodded. "Okay. We'll tackle this together. I'm eager to learn from you."

She took back her hand and there was a pink blush in her cheeks, and it took every ounce of his strength not to take her in his arms and reassure her that everything was going to be okay. That they could do this together, even though he wasn't sure of that.

Working with her in the operating room had given him a false sense of hope and he thought perhaps that nothing had changed between the two of them, but he was wrong. Everything had changed between them and he had to keep reminding himself of that fact.

Maybe they could start again? That thought

scared him. He wasn't sure he could take that chance.

Calum cleared his throat and stood. He wanted to put some distance between them.

"Is George still here?" he asked.

"No. He went back to his place with his mom. I figured we needed to come up with a plan and we could present it to him. I mean, we tried to strategize at The Angry Octopus, but that really didn't work out too well."

"No. It didn't. And there's lots I have to catch you up on. We can try dinner again, but somewhere that's new. Somewhere we don't have any ties to. Somewhere colleagues go all the time and we can work out a plan. Unless you're too tired after that spinal fusion."

He was feeling a bit tired from that surgery, which at six hours had taken longer than he had thought.

"That sounds good. I just want to go home and change."

"I can pick you up."

What're you doing?

Only he knew that she didn't have a vehicle and it was the gentlemanly thing to do.

"Sure." Only her tone didn't sound so sure. "I'll text you my address."

Calum nodded. "About eight? I'm sure I can find a place we can have a late dinner and I'll send you some information about the procedure, and we can go from there."

Pearl nodded. "That sounds good. I'll see you at eight."

Calum nodded and quickly left. He had gone to find Pearl, determined to keep his distance from her, but somehow had made dinner plans with her. What was wrong with him? Why was it when he was around her he forgot all sense?

She got under his skin.

Maybe that's where she'd always been.

CHAPTER FIVE

PEARL WAS STILL in shock that Calum had suggested dinner. She was nervous, but almost secretly pleased.

She didn't care what restaurant. She was just hoping to have a nice meal with a friend.

Is he just a friend?

There was a part of her that didn't think so. She still cared for Calum, but she had ended things between them, and he had made it clear they were just colleagues.

You should have said no.

Only, she had found herself agreeing. She genuinely wanted to learn from Calum and discover his procedures. He had such a high success rate and she had been feeling positive about the whole situation with George after his previous scan, but now she wasn't feeling so sure.

The new scan had terrified her to the very core.

She'd seen osteosarcomas like that and Dr. Chin always amputated, but medicine had come a long way and Calum had had so many successes.

She admired him for that.

She was envious that he was able to forge a new path. What had she done?

You ran away from your feelings, remember?

That's what she did. She'd taken the job offer her father had pressured her to take numerous times and if she was going to waste her surgical career on becoming an orthopedic surgeon over a neurosurgeon or a cardiothoracic surgeon, then she might as well become a private surgeon to a big-league team.

And that's what she'd done.

There was part of her that wanted to leave the job, even though it had been her goal when she became a doctor because she loved the sport, but she couldn't leave. She loved working with the players. They made her feel like part of the team. Their triumphs felt like hers.

When a player returned to the game after she helped them through an injury, it was so satisfying.

She clung to that because the memory of leaving Calum and losing the baby was too much.

The idea of facing Calum was too much. She'd

let him down. And that was a punch to the gut. Every instinct of her was telling her to run.

She was terrified for George. What if this didn't work? What would happen?

You are pessimistic.

And she sighed. Calum was right. She was far too negative.

She had to think positively for George's sake. There was no running from this.

She didn't want to let down George. The team was relying on her. George was relying on her and so was Calum.

Pearl was going to learn from Calum.

She was going to show Calum that she was a damn fine surgeon, too, even if he thought she took the easy way out and left for the lucrative position.

Pearl took a deep calming breath and opened her email to read through the information that Calum had sent her. Tonight at dinner she didn't want to talk about the good old days, she didn't want to reminisce. He had promised her this dinner would be between two colleagues and they would be discussing George and George's care only.

Of course, they'd made promises like that before.

"We're only supposed to study for the boards!" *Calum had said as he took the shot from her.*

"We are studying for the boards. Look, we both have this down pat and you said that I couldn't drink you under the table, so I think that for every wrong answer we take a shot."

Calum laughed. "You're crazy."

"I know, but you know you're the one that was spouting off how you had an iron-clad stomach. So prove it!"

"I know that I do," Calum teased. "You're the one who lost her cool at the board of director's dinner and got up to sing a really bad rendition of that song…some Broadway musical."

Pearl laughed. "I'm a good singer."

Calum had raised an eyebrow. "I can assure you that no hills were alive with the sound of music that night. More like the sound of cat caught in an engine."

Pearl smiled as that memory flitted through her mind.

That foolish drinking game had turned into something more and her blood heated as she thought of that first kiss. That first kiss had made her think of him constantly and then she kissed him again in that on-call room five years ago and that second kiss led to another and another. She closed her eyes and gingerly touched her lips, remembering the feeling of his lips against hers.

No man had ever made her feel that way before and she knew deep down no one ever would, because she wasn't going to open her heart again.

She wasn't going to go through all that pain.

Her life was her career.

And that was it. That was what she'd been taught. Surgery, her medical degree, never let her down.

Pearl sighed and tried to read through the information. She tried to focus on anything that wasn't Calum, but he was like a ghost, haunting her. Always in her thoughts.

Her phone rang and she answered it. "Hello?"

"Pearl?" her mother asked, and Pearl groaned inwardly. Usually she screened her calls from her mother or father. She would call them back when she was able to handle them. When she was able to talk to them and could devote the emotional energy it took to have a conversation with them. But her parents were both narcissists and the conversations were usually one-sided.

"Mom, what can I do for you?" Because that was usually the thrust of the conversation—what Pearl could do for her.

"You're not even going to ask me how I am?" her mother asked indignantly. "I thought I taught you better manners than that."

"Mom, you called me, shouldn't you be asking how I am?"

There were a few moments of silence and Pearl tried not to smile, throwing her mother off on one of her tangents.

"Pearl, I know you're back on the West Coast and I want you to come see me. You have been avoiding me for years. You had the excuse that you were on the East Coast, but you're back here now."

Pearl groaned inwardly. "Mom, I thought you detested guests. They messed with your surgical schedule."

"You're going to visit your father's, aren't you? You always liked him more," she snapped, avoiding Pearl's statement.

"Mom, I'm not a child. I'm a grown woman. And a surgeon."

"I'm a surgeon, too, Pearl."

Pearl sighed. "I can't come to see you, Mom.

I have an extensive case with one of my athletes and I work for a football team now. Autumn is a busy time for the team."

"Extensive case?" her mother asked, piqued.

"Osteosarcoma on a player."

"That's not extensive. You amputate," her mother stated matter-of-factly.

"Mom, you're a cardiothoracic surgeon. Amputation isn't always the solution, like a heart transplant isn't always the solution."

"Every surgeon worth their salt knows that an extensive osteosarcoma can only be truly cured by amputation."

Pearl rolled her eyes and was glad that she wasn't on a video chat with her mother. "I'm working with a surgeon who has developed an intervention. In fact, he won the MSA."

"You're working with Dr. Calum Munro?" her mother asked, impressed. "I didn't know that you knew him."

Seriously, Mom?

She was impressed by Calum's career in orthopedic surgery, but not hers. "Mom, I was engaged to him five years ago. You met him," Pearl said dryly.

"*That's* Dr. Calum Munro who won the MSA?"

"Yes," Pearl said, exasperated. "He's also the man you advised me not to marry. You were quite happy when our engagement ended."

"I never understood why you got engaged in the first place," her mother said, ignoring the obvious facts that Pearl was pointing out. "I've told you time and time again it interferes with your surgical career. If you hadn't been so focused on him five years ago you could've won the MSA by now."

Unbelievable.

This was why Pearl had never told her parents that she was pregnant and lost the child. She had planned to tell them eventually, but she knew they would have said that it was a mistake and that she was throwing away her career. Once she lost the baby, she never saw the need to tell them any different.

It was hers to bear.

She didn't want to share that with her parents. To share that with them would taint it. It would mean sharing her dreams, her longing for the baby, and they would make it something it wasn't. They would try to undermine it, undermine her grief.

Her grandmother had taught her, had given

her the taste of a loving, supportive family. How her father came from such a caring woman, she had never understood, but it was because of her grandmother that she wanted a family.

A real family.

And if her mother or father knew what she wanted they would make her feel like she was a fool.

And she wasn't going to let them in. She wasn't going to do that. She wasn't a fool for wanting love and a career.

"It doesn't matter now, does it?" Pearl said, annoyed. "Mom, I have to go. I have dinner plans. A business dinner."

"Fine. Well, as long as you're not going to see your father in Seattle, then you should stay and do your work." There was a hint of something in her voice. Something that Pearl couldn't quite put her finger on.

"Goodbye, Mom." Pearl disconnected the call and dropped her head in her hands. She suddenly had a pounding headache.

There was a buzz from the intercom and she looked at the clock.

Dammit.

That was most likely Calum and she wasn't

even close to ready. How long had she actually been talking to her mother? How long had she been sitting here, lost in her own thoughts? This was not like her and she hated that she was losing control.

Control was the only thing that kept the grief at bay. Control kept emotions at bay.

She got up and went to the intercom. "Hey."

"Hey, Pearl it's me, Calum. Are you ready?"

"No," she admitted. "I got stuck on a call. Do you want to come up?"

"Sure."

"Great. I'll buzz you in. I'm in the penthouse."

She tried to make herself presentable to answer the door. She was half-undressed, so threw on a robe and ran a brush through her hair. All she had to do was finish her makeup, get dressed and grab her notes, and then she was ready to go.

There was a knock at the door and she peered out the peephole to see Calum. Her heart skipped a beat when she saw him standing there, her body reacting to his presence. She still wanted him, even after all this time. She was still attracted to him.

She might have run from her grief because she thought it was for the best, but she still cared for him. He dressed so well. Like a professional, in a nice suit jacket, pants and a gray sweater.

The gray sweater and the blue suit made his blue eyes even more brilliant, even through the peephole. Her pulse was racing and the butterflies in her stomach were beginning to do the can-can. She was nervous and she had to get control of herself.

She opened the door and he looked her up and down, a smile quirking the corner of his mouth as he saw her in her tattered blue robe.

"Well, that's a little more casual than I expected," he teased.

"Shut up," she groaned, stepping aside to let him in. She shut the door. "I had every intention of being ready, but my mother called."

Calum winced. "Oh, and how is the ice queen of Los Angeles? Does she still hate me?"

Pearl laughed. "Well, she didn't realize that the Dr. Calum Munro of the MSA and the Dr. Calum Munro the cad who wanted to marry her daughter five years ago were the same person."

Calum blinked a couple of times. "Are you serious?"

"When it comes to Moira Henderson I'm always serious," she said sarcastically and then scrubbed a hand over her face.

"Was it that bad?" he asked.

She groaned again. "You know her."

He winced. "Yes. I'm afraid I do. 'You, sir, are a swine!'"

She laughed at him mimicking her mother.

"No one called me 'sir' before," he said.

She cocked an eyebrow. "Yet you've been called swine before?"

"My sister did once. She called me Mr. Swine."

"Why?"

"Oh, I borrowed her blanket for a fort outside, in a rainstorm. It got muddy."

"Ah, hence Mr. Swine."

"Dr. Swine is preferable." There was a twinkle in his eye and she couldn't help but smile.

"It was the semiannual call about visiting her. She just doesn't want my father to have one up her. And it's the same with him. A tug-of-war after all these years."

"I wouldn't know," he sighed. "My father couldn't be bothered with me."

She frowned. "He hasn't changed much. He's only around the team if investors are around. At least he's cordial and nice."

"Well, that's something," Calum snorted.

"Parents are the worst sometimes," she said.

"My mom was good," he admitted. "I miss her."

And she was envious of him. At least he had had one good parent.

"I miss my grandmother," she said wistfully. "She was kind to me. You had your mom longer. She made a good impact on your life."

"That she did," Calum admitted.

"See, that's why you're more optimistic than me."

"Well, then you're forgiven for making me wait," he teased again.

"Have a seat and I'll only be a few moments."

Calum nodded and made his way to her sparsely furnished rental apartment. It was a bit more modern than her taste, but it was clean and bright and would do. It was a place to rest her head at night. It wasn't home. It was just a place to stay while she passed through. Although she didn't want to pass through. Not really. She was tired of that.

Calum wandered around Pearl's apartment. This didn't feel like her place. The place she had before they were together was a bit cozier and eclectic.

Perhaps she's matured?

This apartment felt sterile. Like there was no life here.

It was cold. It reminded him of her mother's home the one time he'd been there.

Is your place any better?

His place was pretty similar. He didn't have much furniture and his house was in shambles. When he wasn't at the hospital he was working on renovations. He had bought it for a steal because it was near the Painted Ladies and in rough shape. After Pearl left him, he needed something to do when he wasn't at the hospital.

He needed to do something with his hands, to keep his mind off the grief, so he had decided to buy the house and slowly fix it up, so he could eventually sell it.

He had a small apartment in the large house where he lived, while the rest of the place was gutted and was a work in progress, but a bedroom, bathroom and kitchen was all he and Max needed. The house had a small fenced yard, but that was perfect for Max to play in and do his business.

There were enough parks nearby that he could take Max for a long walk. And when he had time they'd drive down the coast to the beach or into the redwoods and go on a long hike.

It was perfect for him, though there were days he questioned why he was renovating such a large place. What did he need it for? He didn't plan on getting married or having kids. The pain of losing Pearl and the baby had been too much to bear.

He couldn't lose anyone else. He couldn't go through that again.

So having a big house was a little foolish.

Although there was a part of him, deep down, that had always hoped one day Pearl would come back. That they could get another chance.

It was a foolish dream.

It wasn't really a home, either, but at least his furniture was a lot cozier and comfortable than this modern, white leather stuff.

Calum sat stiffly on the edge of the couch and waited.

He had been second-guessing this invitation out to dinner since he had invited her out to talk about George's case. She had looked so worried about George's scans, so devastated. And he was worried, as well.

He hadn't seen an osteosarcoma like that in a long time.

"I'm ready." Pearl walked from her bedroom and his breath was taken away when he saw her standing there. She was wearing a black dress. It was just a sheath dress and he'd seen that kind of dress before, on other women, but on Pearl it hugged all the right places. She looked sleek and professional.

And the short dress showed off her legs.

Legs that he intimately remembered wrapped around his waist.

Don't think about that now.

"You look great. Much better than the robe," he teased, trying to diffuse the situation and ignore the fact that just the sight of her made him want to take her in his arms and kiss her again.

He longed to kiss her again.

Even after all the hurt. He longed to kiss her one more time. He was losing control again, like he had in the on-call room, when he watched her sleep.

It was hard not to lose control when she was

so beautiful and he keenly remembered what it was like to have her in his arms.

When she was his.

Get a grip on yourself.

"Thanks," she said, and she blushed again. "I didn't have much time to read the information you sent me. I'm sorry, my mother monopolized my time."

"It's fine." And it was. It was a lot of information and he really didn't expect that she would have it all read by now. "I didn't really think that you would have time to read it tonight."

She pulled her coat of her closet and he took it from her, helping her with it. His fingers brushed the nape of her neck, his blood heating.

"Thanks," she said quietly and then took a step back. "Well, I pride myself on doing my due diligence and doing my research. I'm sorry if I let you down."

"You haven't let me down."

At least not in this situation.

He opened the door for her and they left her apartment. They didn't say anything else as they walked down the hall to the elevator.

They stood stiffly, side by side, still not speaking, and he stared at the elevator door.

Not sure what to say. Just listening to the sound of his pulse thundering between his ears and the whir of the elevator going down. It was awkward between them and he hated that it was. The elevator ride down was quick, and his car was out front of the building. He opened the door to his SUV and she slipped inside and sat on a squeaky toy, which let out a horrible sound like a chicken was being murdered.

She shrieked and then pulled out the rubber chicken. "What in the world?"

"I'm sorry. That's one of Max's toys. I thought I got all of them out of the vehicle—apparently I didn't." He was trying so hard not to laugh at her horrified expression.

Pearl was laughing and she gave the rubber chicken another squeeze.

"It sounds awful!"

"Reminds me of your singing," he teased.

Pearl gasped. "Are you again insinuating that I sing like this?"

"What? When?" he asked.

"When we studied for the boards and we were drinking."

He chuckled. "Right. Yeah, I suppose you do."

She tossed the chicken at him and he tossed it

back, so it made that horrible sound again. Pearl rolled her eyes.

"You're so immature," she hissed, teasingly.

Calum laughed. "Perhaps. I would have to get you sing for me again though, but no Broadway music. Please. Don't ruin another one of my favorite things."

"Ha, ha." She threw the rubber chicken into the back seat and Calum shut the door, trying to stop laughing at the look on her face when she sat down on the chicken. That was one thing he always loved about her—she was able to roll with it. She wasn't embarrassed and took something that would potentially irk someone else and laugh about it.

She had a good sense of humor.

He climbed into the driver's side and started the ignition.

"So where are we going?" she asked.

"There's a new bistro down by the wharf. I thought it would be nice to check it out. The view is lovely at night on the bay."

"Sounds good. I always did like it down there."

"You mean down by the bay?" he teased.

"You really haven't changed. You still really make horrible puns," she muttered.

"Is that a pun? I thought it was more like a co-incidental anecdote."

"Fine. Correct me if you want, but if you're not careful I'll sing for you."

Calum laughed. It was so easy to laugh and joke with her, but then other times she was so closed off, so frightened of her feelings. So frightened she ran away, but she was here now. She was back and she wasn't running this time. He was worried she'd leave again, and if she did his heart wouldn't be able to handle it.

This time was different. They were just friends.

Are you so sure about that?

He navigated the windy streets of San Francisco, making his way down to the waterfront and where the small Café Bistro, as it was called, was.

He found a parking spot and they made their way to the restaurant, and their table was waiting for them. They could've had their pick of any of the tables. The place was almost empty.

Pearl made a worried face as they followed the waiter to the corner booth that overlooked the water, where they could comfortably talk about George's case.

After they were seated and the maître d' had left, Pearl leaned over the table.

"Why are we the only ones here?" she whispered, her eyes sparkling in the candlelight. She was trying to hide her amusement.

Calum shrugged. "I don't know."

"This can't be a good sign."

"Don't order any seafood," he teased.

Pearl smiled and laughed under her breath. He hoped this was a good place. He was trying to find a new place that neither one of them had been to. He was trying to find a place that wouldn't bring up any painful memories, but if the food was bad, this place just might invoke some painful memories later.

"So about George," Pearl said. "Please tell me we can try something and we don't have to resort to amputation. Not when his career is just starting."

"I don't know. I really can't predict what will happen, but you know Dr. Chin's feelings on unnecessary surgery when there is no hope."

"The tumor hasn't spread, though. We didn't find any metastasizes."

"I know and that's good." He was hopeful.

"So then there is hope. I understand Dr. Chin's

philosophy and I respect it. I keep to it, if there's no hope and the patient doesn't want it. Why do more harm than good? But if the tumor hasn't spread, can't we try your way?" she asked.

Calum pursed his lips together. "It will be a hard surgery and the radiation will be hard on him. You know one of the effects of radiation is deterioration of the muscles, weakness. Even if we save the leg, he might not be able to play professionally and he needs to come to that re-alization."

Pearl sighed. "I know and we need to have a united front on this. We have to present him with everything and we have to agree."

"We used to agree on a lot of things," Calum said softly.

Pink tinged her cheeks again. "I know..."

"When we worked together it was amazing. We were a force to be reckoned with at that hos-pital."

She smiled, her blue eyes twinkling in the dim light. "Yes. We were quite a team."

And she was right.

It was hard for him to talk about the baby, the grief, the loss. He didn't want to talk about it be-fore, but he did now.

"I missed you when you left," he said.

"I missed you, too."

"Was it just the baby? Is that why you left?"

She worried her bottom lip. "We both had plans, the baby was unexpected and it was hard for me to deal with it."

"It was hard for me, too."

"I know and I'm sorry. I wish I could change the past, but…we both flourished professionally. My parents stayed together and it was awful."

He knew that. She'd told him that before.

"I'm glad you're back, Pearl."

She smiled. "I'm glad I'm back too and that we're working together again."

Calum wanted to ask her what had changed.

"Are you ready to order?" the waiter asked.

"I think so," Calum said. He was never so happy to have a waiter interrupt him before, because he was supposed to be focusing this evening on the patient. On George. Except no matter how hard he tried, when he was with Pearl he forgot everything else and that scared him. He was scared talking about his grief and he was scared of all the old feelings coming back to haunt him.

Sure, he wanted to work with her, but starting things up again? He wasn't so sure about that.

Aren't you?

The last thing that Pearl wanted to do was tell Calum that the food was atrocious and that was probably why no one came here. She didn't want to hurt his feelings when he seemed to be enjoying the dinner.

So when it came time for dessert, she had to pass.

Even though she wouldn't have minded just crossing the street and going to the chocolate store and getting a great big ice-cream sundae with hot fudge sauce. She hadn't indulged in one of those in a long, long time.

"You sure you don't want dessert?" Calum asked.

"Are you going to have some?" she asked skeptically.

"No." And he made a face, which made her chuckle. They split the bill when it came and got the heck out of the Café Bistro as fast as they could.

"I'm so glad that dinner is over," she blurted out.

"You didn't like it?"

"Sorry, no."

"That place should be called the Abysmal Café," he teased.

"So you thought it was awful, too?" she asked.

"Yes, but you seemed to be enjoying yourself."

"I was not. There was so much garlic in my food. So much garlic. It was all I could taste. It's going to take many breath mints to get rid of this. Or some strong liquor."

"My steak was tough. So tough I thought I would have to bathe it in water, like really bathe it in a hot-water bath so that it contained some semblance of moistness."

She wrinkled her nose. "You used that word on purpose."

"What word?"

"Moist. You know I hate that word."

"Why does everyone hate that word?" he asked.

"We've had this conversation too many times to get into it again."

"Fine. Do you want some ice cream then? Because I can't stop picturing a nice ice-cream sundae and we're down here by the water."

"I would love that."

It was an odd thing to go for an ice-cream

sundae in late October, but it felt like old times. Joking and talking about things they used to talk about and going to get ice cream. They both found a table in the ice-cream shop located in an old factory. There were heat lamps on the patio and they sat outside, having ice cream in the autumn.

"This is so much better than that dinner," she said, taking a scoop of ice cream.

"Agreed. I haven't done this in forever."

"Same. I mean, there was a good fake frozen yogurt thing in New York City, but it was nothing compared to this."

"Fake frozen yogurt?" he asked, horrified.

"Yeah, some kind of whipped thing. Nothing like this." What was she doing? Why was she letting herself fall into this trap again? Why was it so easy with Calum? He made her feel like she was a carefree resident again. He got through all her barriers. It was fun and easy and so exciting with him.

She needed to change the subject fast.

"Shall we talk to George and his mother tomorrow?" she asked soberly. Talking about George and work was a safe, neutral buffer. A chance to keep him and the memories he evoked at bay.

Calum nodded. "The sooner we get started, the better. How about I come to the training facility first thing in the morning?"

"That sounds good." She finished up her ice cream. "Thank you for talking me through everything and I appreciate that you're going to try and help him."

"I will do my best, Pearl, but if it gets too much and if it spreads…" Calum trailed off and he didn't say anything else. She knew what he was getting at.

She knew that George's career would be over before it started and she couldn't imagine that. To have a dream taken away from you.

Can't you?

And just that realization made a lump form in the pit of her stomach as she thought of her baby. It had never really been a dream of hers, but once she'd gotten used to the idea that she was going to be a mother it had all been taken from her.

She couldn't hold on to it.

The moment she lost the baby it was as though a knife had torn her heart into shreds. All her dreams had been shattered. She had no control over that moment, no control over her body not being able to hold on.

She had been powerless and it terrified her.

Even though she knew medically why she miscarried, there was an irrational part of her that made her think that maybe she didn't want it enough and therefore didn't deserve it. Although she knew that thought was foolish, it was there, in the darkest recesses of her inner dialogue, because the baby had been unplanned, because she wasn't ready and because her own birth had ruined her parents lives.

And she hated herself for thinking like that.

"Well, I should get back. I have to talk to George's coach and make sure that he's there at the training facility first thing."

Calum nodded and they both got up, discarded the empty plastic containers and walked back to his car.

The moon was high in the sky. Large and orange. A harvest moon. She took a moment to stare up at it, rising over the bay and the iconic Golden Gate Bridge. The lights of the city shimmered across the water and there was a low fog drifting across the surface.

It was silent, standing here right now. She'd forgotten how magical this city could be.

She forgot how many memories it brought back.

Good and bad. The good times were with her grandmother and the trips to the wharf or to a football game. The bad times were losing the baby and leaving Calum.

She was a fool.

"So did that sundae help get rid of the garlic?" he asked.

"Perhaps."

He turned and faced her, then took her hands, and her heart began to race as she stood there with him, not sure what was going to happen.

"Well, let's see." He touched her face and before she could stop herself she closed her eyes and melted into his arms kissing him, like no time had passed.

Like they hadn't changed.

And her emotions began to overtake her.

If she didn't put a stop to it, she was going to lose all control and she couldn't lose control. Pearl pushed Calum away. She panicked. She wanted that kiss, but she couldn't get caught up with him again. They were supposed to stay friends. Nothing more.

"You know what, I'll just take a cab home."

"What?" he asked, confused.

"Good night, Calum." And she turned and left him standing there.

Running again.

CHAPTER SIX

PEARL HATED BREAKING the news to George.

She hated this part of the job and seeing his face fall as she and Calum told him was so difficult, but he had to know all his options. He had to know what kind of treatment he was going to go through, what the repercussions were and the fact that they might not be able to do anything.

George looked broken and his mother held his hand. She was holding back tears.

"I'm so sorry, George," Pearl said gently. "You need to know your choices."

George stared at the table, looking lost. She knew that feeling well. She knew how it felt when your life was shattered, when all your hopes and dreams were dashed because your body, your health, failed you.

"So it's grown again. Really fast?" George asked.

"Yes," Calum said. "It's an aggressive tumor and when I get in there and do a biopsy I'll be able to determine which medication regimen to start you on, but we need to start treatment as soon as possible, if that's the course of action you wish to take."

George nodded, then was quiet for a moment. "And the other option is…"

"We amputate," Pearl said. "I'm so sorry, George."

"Would amputation cure his cancer?" George's mother asked.

"Yes, it would remove the cancer. So far the cancer hasn't spread, but even if we amputate we need to do a round of chemotherapy to make sure that it doesn't return."

"Baby, why don't we do the amputation?" George's mother asked, but it was more like she was pleading with him.

"Mom, I'm not getting the amputation. I want to fight this," George said fiercely.

Calum leaned forward. "Very well, George, but you do understand that I have never done my treatment on someone with such an advanced osteosarcoma. If the treatment fails, you will still need the amputation and you'll be much weaker. Even if the treatment works, you could be left very weak."

George nodded. "I understand, Doc, but I have to try."

Calum nodded. "Okay. Well, then I want to start treatment right away. I will contact the hospital and have you admitted. We're going to start with a biopsy so that I know how to target it."

George nodded and then looked at his mom. "It'll be okay, Mom. You can go back to Philly."

"I'm not going anywhere. Your brothers and sister are old enough now and they're being taken care of. Don't you worry. My place is here with you."

Pearl felt a pang of jealously. She certainly didn't have that kind of relationship with her own parents. The only person who had loved her like that was her grandmother.

And Calum.

She tried not to think of their kiss last night and how she had fled. It was the only way she could get control of herself. That kiss had thrown her off-kilter. It brought back everything and she was scared what Calum stirred in her.

"Come on, let's get to the hospital so I can beat this cancer's ass!" George said brightly.

"George! Don't swear in front of the doctors," his mother admonished.

Calum laughed and walked over to hold open the door so that George's mother could wheel him out of the boardroom where they were meeting.

"I've heard worse," Calum teased. "I'll see you in a couple of hours. No more eating or drinking okay?"

"Will do, Doc." George shook Calum's hand and was wheeled out of the room. Calum shut the door behind him.

"That was hard," Pearl sighed.

"No harder than last night?"

Pearl bit her lip. "Calum, about last night… we're supposed to be colleagues. It caught me off guard."

His expression softened. "I'm sorry about what happened. I didn't mean to kiss you…it threw me off guard, too."

"It's okay. What's done is done."

"So I take it you're coming to watch me do a biopsy?" he asked.

"Of course," Pearl said quickly. "If you're all right with that."

"It's okay. Are you okay?"

"I'm fine," she said, although she wasn't too

sure. "You don't have to keep asking me if I'm okay."

The truth was, she wasn't okay. After their horrible dinner and then ice-cream date, she had once again been tossing and turning all night, berating herself for allowing herself to fall into old patterns with Calum.

She was worried that she was falling for him again. Who was she kidding? She'd never stopped caring for him.

Why was it that she couldn't control herself when she was around him?

Why did she allow herself to slip into these old habits? Why had she let him kiss her?

The thing was she wanted that kiss and when it came to Calum she had no self-control. She got swept up in good memories, happy times, even love.

"Okay, I'll stop," Calum said. "We have a plan in place and we can do this, but you look tired."

"Right," Pearl said quickly. "I am tired. I just didn't have a good night's sleep. I was worried about breaking the news to George."

Not a complete lie—she was worried about that—but she didn't want him to know that he was the reason she was a bit off. That she was feeling tense being alone with him, that he was getting through her barriers and that's because she really didn't want to keep him out, but she was afraid of letting him in. She was afraid of getting hurt, of hurting him. It was easier for her to keep this as she intended, as friends.

One thing was for certain is that she had to get out of San Francisco for a bit and that's why when she got home after her dinner with Calum she texted Dianne and accepted her invitation to the ranch for the weekend. She just needed to get away for a couple of days.

She needed to put some space between her and Calum.

And be in a place that her parents couldn't find her and manipulate her with their toxic one-upmanship and their perpetual disappointment that she didn't follow in their respective specialties.

That her life was not the life they wanted or expected of her.

Truth be told, her life wasn't exactly how she pictured it. She just needed to get away from it all. She needed to put things in perspective.

Running again.

She shook away that thought.

"He's informed, he's an adult and he's made his decision. It will be good to have you at the biopsy," Calum said, interrupting her thoughts.

"Do you want to get some air?" Pearl asked.

"Sure."

"Let's go. I have to go down to the field and check a couple of players, anyway. They're not playing right now, but the coach wants them on the roster. I have to see a couple of them before they go out on the road."

"Sure."

Calum, ever the gentleman, held open the door for her and they walked out of the boardroom. Pearl led him through the facility and then down to the field, where the Bridgers were out running drills.

The players she wanted to see were on the sidelines.

"Do you want me to come down on the field?" he asked.

"Sure. Why not? You can help."

He nodded. "Okay. I don't know how much help I can be, though. You've dealt with orthopedic injuries."

"You can help, come on."

They headed down onto the field and over to the sidelines, where the players were waiting.

They waved as she approached them.

And she was met with greetings of "hey, Doc" and "what's up, Doc."

"Dr. Calum Munro, this is the lead quarterback, Jose Fernandez. He's taken one too many blows recently and broken a few ribs."

"Pleasure to meet you, Dr. Munro," Jose said as he held out his hand, which was taped. Pearl frowned when she saw that and gingerly took his hand.

"What have you been doing?" she demanded.

Jose shrugged. "I got tackled pretty bad in the last game. I'm still recovering from that concussion from last month. Anyways, I lost my balance and was open for the tackle. I bent a couple of fingers back."

"Concussions can take weeks to heal, Jose." She looked at his hand.

"I know, Doc. I thought I was fine, though."

"Have you gone to get this X-rayed?" she asked.

Jose sighed. "Not yet, Doc. I swear I was on my way up."

Pearl gave him a stern look and then stepped

aside for Calum to look. "What do you think, Dr. Munro?"

Calum took Jose's hand. "Definitely dislocated a joint. There's swelling. You did a good job taping though, Jose. I should've benched you, but it didn't look this bad last night."

"Thanks, Doc!" Jose said brightly. "It was fine during the game, but I finished practice today and it's worse. It's a bit tender."

"You need to get up and see Marta in X-ray. I want to see how badly you've dislocated your joints and I want to make sure there isn't any tendon damage in your arm. Your *good* throwing arm."

"Yes, Doc." Jose made his way off the field.

"You talk to them like you're their mother," Calum teased.

"I guess I am in a way, but they need to take care of their injuries and not play through the pain, but no matter how much I talk about that, they do. They're professional athletes."

"I get that," Calum said.

"Do you?" she asked, crossing her arms.

"Sure. Aren't surgeons like that in some way? We work grueling long hours, sometimes ignoring what our body is telling us. We don't eat, we don't sleep as we fight for our patients' lives."

"You're right, although my parents wouldn't agree with you."

He was confused. "Aren't they surgeons, too?"

"Yes, but they see their surgery is something legitimate. Orthopedic surgeons aren't as important as a cardiothoracic surgeon or a neurosurgeon as far as they are concerned. You can live without a leg, but you can't live without a heart or a brain...though my parents seem to be doing a good job of that."

"Are you serious?" he asked.

"I think I have told you this before."

"Right. I tend to block out memories of your mother," he teased.

She laughed. "Can't blame you for that."

"I don't understand why they hated your choice in surgery."

"Because it's not theirs. Although, my father respects my job working with the Bridgers."

"Why?" Calum asked.

"Money." She regretted it instantly the moment she said it. Like her answer was confirming something.

"I guess that's something," he said firmly. "My

father, who was absent most of my childhood, felt like I should become an investor like him. Of course, that's only when I grew older and showed an aptitude for figures. When I was a kid, he couldn't be bothered with me."

"I'm sorry that I've forced you to come here. I forgot about your relationship with your dad momentarily."

"What relationship?" Calum shrugged. "It doesn't matter that Grayson Munro, one of the major investors of this team, is my father."

She knew Grayson Munro, he was very persuasive—Calum's father had encouraged her to do whatever it took to save George's career because he had personally invested so much in George's career with the Bridgers.

Had Grayson worked some deal with Calum? Perhaps Calum really didn't want to help her because he cared about George and about the case. Maybe he had no choice.

"Is that why you're helping me?" she asked.

Calum cocked an eyebrow. "What're you talking about?"

"Your father is an investor for the Bridgers. Is he the one that forced you to take on my case?"

* * *

Calum was stunned that that was the first thing she would think about. Did she really think so little of him? His father might have invested in the Bridgers, but he hadn't come to Calum and asked him for help. Why was she always looking for something to push him away?

Why were you?

"Pearl, I don't talk to my father. He had nothing to do with this."

She pursed her lips together. "I believe you."

"I've never lied to you, Pearl. You know I don't talk to him."

"I know. I'm sorry."

He knew she had trust issues, but he was glad she believed him. He had never lied to her.

Of course, he wasn't telling her everything. He wasn't telling her that kiss last night scared him, that her walking away hurt him, but was also a relief.

Being with her made him lose all control. It was like no time had passed between them. He forgot who he was when he had her in his arms.

And suddenly, he was very thankful that he was getting out the city for the weekend. Max was going his to favorite doggy day-care place and he was going to just get away, into the mountains for some peace and quiet.

Away from this.

All of these emotions. He had been overcome when he kissed her. He'd forgotten everything. When he was with Pearl he forgot what happened. The pain when she left.

Kissing her, he lost all control.

He still cared for her.

He still loved her, but he couldn't open up to her. When she left him last night, he remembered why he guarded his heart.

"I really am thankful that you're assisting me. There's no one I would rather have."

He nodded, but he wasn't so sure about that, not really. If she really wanted him why had she left all those years ago?

"Well, I think I'm going to head back to the hospital," he said, because he didn't really have much more to say. Not at this time.

Not without saying something that he would regret.

Would you regret it, though?

"Sure. I will be there as soon as I check up on Jose's hand."

"Make sure there isn't a crush injury," he added.

She gave him a look that said "please" and then he chuckled softly. He'd forgotten who he was talking to.

"I'll see you later," she said over her shoulder, heading back into the facility.

Calum headed in the opposite direction, watching the players on the field, taking his time as he processed everything. All the emotions he was feeling, how it was so easy to get wrapped back up in Pearl's life and why he was a lost man when it came to Pearl Henderson.

"Calum!"

Hearing his name, Calum spun around and his stomach twisted as he saw his father up in the stands, not far from him.

It had been a long time since he had seen Grayson Munro, at least as long as he and Pearl had split up. And honestly, although it felt like an eternity that he and Pearl had been apart, it didn't quite feel long enough since he had last seen his father.

"Father," Calum said stiffly.

His father was still decked out in one of his expensive tailored suits and when he saw those suits all he could think about is how his mother barely scraped by and sometimes didn't have food for herself to feed them.

His father's dark hair was almost white and Calum was thankful that he took after his mother and her ginger coloring.

There weren't many ways he resembled his father. A few traits, but there was nothing but a name connecting Dr. Calum Munro with Grayson Munro.

"What're you doing here, son?"

Grayson never called him "son" unless there were people around and his father was putting on a show. As Calum scanned the bleachers, he saw there were a group of people farther up, sitting politely, so that was why his father was putting on a performance. He had no doubt that they were a group of investors.

"Laying it on thick, eh, Father?"

Grayson was not amused with that, but he didn't let the saccharine act slip. "I'm surprised to see you here, son. Why don't you come up and say hi to some people? I've been telling them all about my son who won the most prestigious medical award."

"Another time." Calum waved to the group,

all of whom were looking at him. "I'm wanted back at the hospital."

"Surely that can wait? What kind of emergency case is an orthopedic surgeon needed for?"

Calum narrowed his eyes. "Actually, it's for one of your star players. George Vaughn. He has a pretty bad osteosarcoma and your team's surgeon contacted me to help him out with that ground-breaking surgery that I won the award for. He's waiting for me at the hospital."

Grayson was stunned. "I had no idea it was that bad."

"It is. So when I say another time, I mean another time," he said tightly.

"I'll call you later, son. Take care of our star player." Grayson turned and headed up the bleachers to the investors, and Calum watched him kowtowing and kissing ass in disgust.

His father only let him go without fighting because there was a crowd watching and because the patient was someone he was personally invested in.

And by invested in, Calum meant financially invested in.

If it had been anyone else and they had been alone, Calum knew that his father would have raised more of a stink. Calum and his mother were always supposed to jump whenever Grayson Munro graced them with his presence. His mother had been so in love with Grayson, even after he left, that she had always hoped he'd come back.

Right up until her death. She had held out hope he'd return. Only he hadn't.

And Grayson certainly liked to throw it in Calum's face that he had paid for his education and that Calum owed him.

Even though Calum had told Pearl the truth, that his father hadn't put him up to this, he hoped that taking care of George would repay the supposed debt that he owed his father.

This was why Calum had never really wanted a family.

Never wanted to get married.

He didn't have a good role model, but when Pearl had told him he was pregnant, he had been willing to give it a shot, because he loved Pearl that much. He wanted Pearl and he wanted their child. He thought maybe he could have happiness, and the longer they were together, the more hopeful he had become for a family life he'd never had.

Pearl had made his life better.

Calum had sworn from the moment that Pearl told him that she was pregnant that he was never going to be like his father and he was going to strive to do better.

He would do better.

Of that he was certain, only that chance had been taken away from him when they lost the baby, and Calum was too worried about the pain of ever trying again.

One thing was for certain, one thing he knew—he would never prioritize a patient because of money.

He was not that coldhearted.

"Can you feel that, George?" Calum asked as he tested the skin around where he was going to make the biopsy incision. He'd given George an epidural, because he couldn't wait the full six hours for George to have a completely empty stomach and put him under general anesthesia.

So he and Pearl had decided that it would be best if George had an epidural.

"I can't feel anything, Doc," George said from behind the surgical drape.

"Good." Calum looked over at Pearl, who was

standing on the opposite side of the table. She was there for moral support for George, who was trembling, but that was the effect of the epidural.

"You're doing great, George," Pearl encouraged.

"Yeah, but I'm the only player going through all this junk and surgery."

"Jose crushed a couple of fingers. I admitted him just before I came in here."

"What?" George asked, staring up at Pearl.

Calum chuckled because he knew that Pearl, who usually didn't talk about patient-confidentially stuff, was trying to take George's mind off the fact that he was starting a rough journey treating his cancer.

And he also knew that Jose had given Pearl permission to talk to George about it because Jose also wanted to ease George's mind off the fact he was going to have his leg, the thing that helped carry him to the very cusp of his dream, be put through the ringer.

"How did he crush his hand?" George asked.

"During the game yesterday. What we thought was a sprain was a lot worse. He's still recovering from that concussion, so he's a bit out of it. He's benched for a while. I have to tell you your coach is not happy having you out this season and Jose out for a couple months, at least. He needs surgery."

"No, I suppose he's not happy." George re-laxed, which was the best thing for him. Pearl was keeping George's mind off the leg. She might have been called an ice queen when they were residents, but that was the furthest thing from the truth.

She was kind to her patients and he understood why she liked her job. The players relied on her and she treated them like they were her kids.

She was concerned about them. She cared for them.

Although she tried to hide it, there was a soft side to Dr. Pearl Henderson.

He knew first-hand what it was like to have her melt in his arms and under his touch.

Calum was handed the scalpel so that he could start his incision, so he could take a piece of the tumor that was invading George's bone.

And he wanted to get a good look at it close up, under his microscopes. He wanted to know what he was up against so that he could help George.

"Hey, Doc Munro, have you started?" George asked.

"He has," Pearl said. "But if you bug him too much he might slip!"

"I never slip," Calum muttered and then winked at George.

George was laughing. "It's kind of quiet in here. Don't you have some music or something? I'm going stir-crazy."

"Well, our teacher used to like to listen to Queen when he was doing surgery," Pearl said. "It annoyed Calum and he likes it quiet."

"Why?" George asked. "Doc, that's seriously boring."

"Sure, get the patient on your side, Dr. Henderson," Calum teased.

Pearl's eyes were twinkling. He loved being here in the operating room with her. This felt right. This felt like they belonged together. They worked well together. She anticipated his moves. She knew what he needed done before he had to ask. They moved and thought like one. They were partners. They were equals and he missed this.

"I'll always side with the lady, Dr. Munro. Sorry about that."

Calum laughed softly as he dissected down to where he needed to take a sample from. "In this case, I don't blame you. Dr. Henderson is not bad on the eyes."

"No, indeed." George's eyes rolled back into his head.

"George?" Pearl asked, her voice rising. "George, stay with me."

"His blood pressure is bottoming out," Dr. Knox, the anesthesiologist, stated. "I'll hang some more fluid. It's common with an epidural."

Pearl nodded, but Calum could tell she was a bit worried.

"Surely, this isn't your first patient that's had a reaction to an epidural?" Calum asked.

"Usually my patients are under general anesthesia. I have yet to do a knee replacement under an epidural," she said.

"I have," Calum said. "Not the most pleasant thing for the patient. I do prefer general anesthesia, but a couple of years ago we had a patient who was allergic to the medication and an epidural was our only option."

"I'm envious," Pearl said.

"Of what?" Calum asked.

"You have a bigger scope of cases here. More than I do."

"Well, I didn't leave," he said tersely.

He knew that he had hurt her, and he hadn't meant for that to slip out, but it was the truth. She had left for a higher-paying job, but one that was so stifled in the scope of cases. He saw everything an orthopedic surgeon could see here in the hospital, which is why he had been so successful developing his treatment plan.

Pearl didn't say anything else as George came to.

"Whoa, is it over?" he asked weakly.

"Almost," Calum said. "Just a few more minutes."

He glanced up at Pearl, but she was focused on George, her back to him. He knew that he had hurt her, but she had hurt him, too.

Still, he hated himself right in this moment.

He hated himself for hurting her, which was the last thing he wanted to do.

CHAPTER SEVEN

PEARL TOOK A deep breath when she got off the last train in downtown Sonora. It had been a long day, but the train journey gave her time to catch up on work and to think about everything. She'd been hurt when Calum had said what he did during George's biopsy, but she couldn't blame him.

He was right. She'd run away. She'd hurt him. Every day she regretted that decision from five years ago.

After George was stabilized, she went to check on Jose and talk over the surgery she wanted to do on him and then she prepped for that, while avoiding Calum.

She performed Jose's surgery and George started his targeted radiation on Thursday, and she got on the train on Friday.

Calum had been avoiding her and she was okay with that.

She'd been avoiding him, too. After that kiss. She knew she had to put distance between them and going away to Dianne's was the perfect escape from all the ghosts of San Francisco.

She made sure that everything back in San Francisco was wrapped up and taken care of before she boarded her first, of several, trains to Sonora, California, where she was looking forward to the time out in the country, away from the city, away from her parents and most especially away from Calum.

Sonora was a six-hour train ride, but it didn't feel far enough.

"Pearl!"

Pearl turned and saw that Dianne was waiting in the parking lot of the train station. Pearl sighed in relief and made her way through the crowd and over to Dianne, where she got a big hug. It made her feel welcome and at home, like it always did. She'd forgotten.

"I'm so glad you decided to come and that you survived the train ride. You seriously need to get a car!" Dianne teased.

"I like traveling by train. I could work, but I'm glad to be here. I'm looking forward to a hot shower and a change of clothes."

"Of course. And Jerome is barbecuing."

"In late October?" Pearl asked, stunned.

"You forget you're on the West Coast. It's not freezing as New York City is."

"It's October. It's not *that* cold."

Although they had the odd strange snowfall.

She would miss New York in the snow. She always did like seeing Central Park covered in snow, but she definitely wouldn't miss the crowds and the bone-chilling cold of a New York winter. She much preferred California.

"Thanks again for having me. You saved me from having to spend another weekend alone."

"No problem. I've missed you and video chatting or texting isn't the same as being together."

They climbed into Dianne's Jeep. Dianne drove away from the train station and through the small California town, although Dianne and Jerome didn't really live in Sonora proper—it was just the closest town that Pearl could get to. Their little village Mountain Spring was part of the greater Sonora area, but not in the city limits.

Dianne and Jerome's ranch was closer to the hills. It was nestled in the foothills with lots of trees and Pearl couldn't wait to go for a nice long walk out on their trails, just to clear her head and not think about Calum.

She was so glad that he was back in San Francisco and she was here. Ever since she'd returned to San Francisco, all she thought about was Calum and it was driving her crazy. She could not stop thinking about the kiss and everywhere in San Francisco brought back memories of their time together.

So many ghosts in San Francisco. She needed a ghost-free weekend to collect her thoughts.

"So your mom was bugging you again?" Dianne asked, breaking through Pearl's thoughts.

"She always is."

"You know, you're an adult. You don't have to deal with her."

"I know, but both my parents find a way to annoy me."

"You're too nice," Dianne said softly. "You're an excellent surgeon and you don't put up with a lot of crap, but you're too nice to them."

"I know. They couldn't give a crap about each other or anyone else. They're both so selfish. In retrospect, I should've ended up that way. But, honestly, they embarrassed me so much when I was a kid, I just didn't want to be like that."

"I understand. Family has a way of pulling on you, from different directions. It's all well and good to dump those toxic members from your life, but they make up the fabric of your existence and it's hard to pull away one thread."

Pearl nodded. It was true.

There were some people in your life that just became a part of you and no matter how much you tried to pull away, they were there, binding you to them. Pearl was just going to have deal with the fact that Calum was an important part of her past and that she'd always be drawn to him.

She would just have to cope with that, and as much as she wanted him to be a part of her life, he couldn't. She was too afraid of what would happen.

The rest of the drive out to Dianne's ranch was enjoyable. Dianne talked about her new job and Jerome's practice and what Derek was up to as a rambunctious five-year-old.

As they pulled up to the log house at the end of the long winding drive, Pearl's heart skipped a beat when she recognized a familiar SUV in the drive, one with San Francisco plates. Her stomach knotted and dropped to the soles of her feet.

"Dianne?" she asked, hoping her voice didn't shake.

Dianne worried her bottom lip, her big brown

eyes wide. "I know. I'm sorry, but he comes every couple of months."

"I wish you would've have told me."

"You wouldn't have come and you would've been miserable in San Francisco. Besides, I saw the two of you in that surgery a few days ago and you were both fine. I didn't think you'd mind."

Dianne got out of the car and Pearl just sat there for a moment letting it all sink in. Yes, she and Calum had got along fine during that surgery that Dianne had assisted on, but she hadn't been there for George's biopsy. Or for that kiss and the way she had run from Calum again.

Dianne didn't know how he'd embarrassed her with that comment, not that she could blame him.

It was just the fact it was in front of other hospital staff.

You can handle this. This ranch is big enough for the both of you.

Only she wasn't too sure about that. She got out of the car and picked up her suitcase. The front door opened and Jerome came out.

"I didn't quite believe it when she told me you were coming!" Jerome came over to her and enfolded her in a big bear hug, giving her a kiss on the cheek. "I've missed you, *chica*. It's been way too long."

"It has." Pearl gave him a kiss back. "Where's Derek? I have something for him from New York."

"He's asleep. He got tired of waiting." Jerome took her suitcase and Pearl followed him and Dianne up the steps into the main foyer of their beautiful log cabin.

Pearl was taken aback by the high ceilings and the rustic feeling of the place, but also impressed with the modern amenities she could see as the space was open concept.

"Pearl?"

Pearl spun around and saw that Calum was on the stairs. He'd been coming down the main staircase and paused on the landing when he saw her.

"Hi, Calum," she said, hoping that Jerome and Dianne didn't notice the tension.

"I didn't know you were coming," Calum said, coming down the stairs. He had a strange expression on his face and she knew that he was trying to make sure that Jerome and Dianne didn't know that he was just as shocked and uncomfortable as she was.

"I didn't know you'd be here, either," she said quietly.

"I come every year around this time," Calum stated.

"He helped with a lot of the construction on this place over the last few years," Jerome said. "He is an amazing woodworker."

Pearl raised her eyebrows. "Wow. I had no idea."

"No, why would you?" Calum asked quietly.

"Come on," Dianne said, stepping between them, and from her really large smile, Pearl knew that Dianne was sensing some of the tension. "Let me show you to your room, Pearl. You probably want to freshen yourself up before Jerome tries to poison you with his homemade beer."

Dianne took the suitcase from Jerome.

"Hey!" Jerome teased and Calum was laughing.

Pearl followed Dianne up the stairs. She turned to look over her shoulder briefly and saw that Calum was watching her go up the stairs.

This was going to be a *long* weekend indeed.

When Pearl had cleaned up and changed her clothes, she headed downstairs. She was tired from her train trip and it was late, but she was hungry. Train food was okay, but when she got out of the shower she could smell Jerome's barbecue all the way from her room and her stomach was growling.

Everyone was in the kitchen area around the main island. There were wineglasses out and Calum was laughing and talking with Dianne and Jerome. And suddenly, she felt out of place with her friends. Like she didn't belong.

Like she was the interloper. She was so unnerved she almost turned around and went back upstairs.

You were invited.

Dianne wanted her here and she wanted to see Derek again. She walked into the kitchen, feeling awkward.

"Hey," she said brightly.

"Pearl, would you like a glass of wine?" Dianne asked.

"Yes. As long as Jerome didn't make it," Pearl teased.

Dianne laughed and pulled out a glass, pouring her a glass of red.

"I have to say, Pearl, I'm quite hurt that you don't trust my ability to brew beer or make wine.

I mean, I have a kit and everything," Jerome stated.

Dianne raised her eyebrows and shook her head subtly as she took a sip. Pearl tried not to laugh.

"Maybe some other time, Jerome. I've been on a train all day and I don't want to risk anything after eating train food," Pearl said.

"Fair enough." Jerome headed out to the back deck, where she could see smoke rising from the large built-in gas barbecue.

"I'm going to see if he needs help," Dianne said, quickly scurrying after her husband and leaving Pearl and Calum alone.

"I'm sorry if I'm ruining your plans," Pearl said quickly. "If I had known you were coming I wouldn't have intruded."

Calum sighed. "No, I'm sorry. I didn't mean to say what I said the other day in the biopsy."

"Apology accepted. Your kiss threw me off and I panicked."

Calum sighed. "It threw me off, too. Pearl, I'm okay that you're here. You and Dianne are best friends. We can be adults—I mean, we are working together on George's case and this place is definitely big enough for the both of us."

She wanted to believe him, but she somehow doubted that this place was big enough for both of them. San Francisco didn't seem to be a big enough expanse for the two of them, but if he was willing to make this work, she was willing to make this work.

"Do you think this was a setup?" she asked.

Calum nodded. "I don't know what she's playing at. I think she's longing for the good old days."

"You mean when we were all broke and tired, making our way through residency?"

Calum smiled. "Yeah, that."

"Life seemed simpler then, from this perspective, anyway."

"Yes. That's for sure. So you avoided visiting your mother, huh?"

"Of course, I'm the master of that," she teased.

"You know, I have met your father."

"When?" she asked.

Calum chuckled. "I have. I met your father when I won the award, actually. He's not the most... He's not very warm and personable."

"That's a polite way of putting it," she said dryly.

"You never told him about me, did you?" he asked.

"I did, but he couldn't care less. It was just my mother who said I was throwing my life away, but now you're a catch." Heat bloomed in her cheeks as she said that. She hadn't meant to, even if it was the truth.

There was a twinkle in his eye as he leaned over the island. "So I'm a catch, eh?"

Pearl rolled her eyes and tried not to laugh. "You're only a catch to my mother because you won that prestigious award and are a brilliant surgeon. Of course, when I wanted to marry you, you weren't worth my time and would ruin my life."

"Did you?"

"Did I what?" Pearl asked.

"Did you want to marry me?" he asked gently.

Pearl's face bloomed pink again and his own pulse was thundering in his ears. When she blushed like that, it made his heart skip a beat.

Why did he still want her? He just couldn't resist her. He had never gotten over her and he doubted he ever could.

He waited for an answer. Not that he really

expected to hear what he really wanted and he wasn't sure what that was. She was the one who had left him.

She had left him, like so many people in his life had done before. His dad, his sister and even his mom left him, in a way, when she died. But Pearl made him feel alive again. She always had. He had only ever wanted her. He still wanted a life with her.

"Calum…" She blushed again. "I…"

He reached over and took her hand. It was small and delicate, just like he remembered. He'd admired her hands many times when they were doing work. She had surgeon hands, but they were still soft and fit so well in his.

Her breath hitched in her throat and he took a step closer to her. He didn't know what he was expecting in this moment. She hadn't answered his question and he didn't care. He just wanted to be close to her again.

She looked up at him, her lips parted, and he ran his thumb over her cheek.

God, he wanted to kiss her again. He couldn't resist her. Why couldn't he resist her?

"You don't have to say anything," he whispered.

"It's not that, it's…"

"It's what?"

"I think the ribs are finally done," Dianne said, coming back into the kitchen.

Pearl pulled her hand away and took another sip of her wine, and Calum stepped back. Dianne paused and looked at them both.

"Is everything okay?" Dianne asked, confused.

"Perfectly fine." It was a lie—there was something unfinished here and he'd been so close to her. So close to finally getting through to her after all these years.

"We were just discussing our case back in San Francisco. The young linebacker for the Bridgers," Pearl said.

"No work talk," Dianne moaned. "This is supposed to be a fun weekend."

"Can I help you with anything?" Pearl asked, following Dianne from the kitchen into the dining room.

Calum tried not to sigh in regret. He was annoyed they had been interrupted. He just wanted to kiss her again. He hadn't stopped thinking about the kiss.

Maybe it was good Dianne had come in before he got too carried away.

Calum abandoned his glass of wine and headed out on the deck, where Jerome was finishing up with the cooking.

"You okay?" Jerome asked as Calum wandered out onto the deck.

"I'm fine."

Which was a lie.

He stood at the edge of the deck and stared up at the sky. The stars were out and the night was clear and crisp. It was cooler here than in San Francisco. It was kind of perfect and he understood why this had been Dianne and Jerome's dream.

"You're clearly not fine," Jerome said.

"And how do you figure that?"

Jerome shook his head. "I've known you more than a decade. You try to hide stuff, you try to bottle up your emotions, but I know something is bothering you. You surgeons think you're made of steel, and that you're emotionless automatons that can deal with whatever, but every surgeon I've met is moody, with a capital moo."

Calum cocked an eyebrow. "What?"

"I can say that because I'm not a surgeon. I was an anesthesiologist and now I'm a family doctor.

I'm not a surgeon, therefore I can express myself a lot better."

Calum snorted. "Oh, yeah? And when are you going to tell Dianne about that big-screen television that you bought, the one that's as big as her living room wall?"

Jerome shot him a look. "That's neither here nor there."

"You're hiding it from her."

"I'll eventually tell her. Are you going to tell Pearl about how you feel?"

Calum frowned. His stomach twisted in a knot, because Jerome had hit the nail on the head. He wasn't sure that he was going to ever tell Pearl how he felt. Too much time had passed. Maybe it was too late for them.

"Exactly my point," Jerome stated. "Calum, why don't you just talk to her?"

"I will…soon. Right now we have to work on an important case together and we just have to keep it professional. That's the best we can do right now."

Calum knew by Jerome's face that he didn't believe him, but Jerome was a good enough friend that he wasn't going to push Calum. Jerome had been here when Calum was grieving—not only the loss of the baby, but also the loss of Pearl.

"Okay, man. I won't say anything else. Let's go eat some ribs!"

Calum nodded. "Sounds good."

He held open the door for Jerome and followed him inside.

He couldn't let himself slip like that, but when he was around Pearl he lost all sense of reason.

CHAPTER EIGHT

CALUM CAME DOWN later than he intended to, but he had had a horrible night's sleep. Usually, he slept pretty well at Dianne and Jerome's place, but he couldn't get Pearl out of his head. All he could think about was her, how close he'd been and how it felt to touch her. How it felt to kiss her again.

And how she was down the hall. He thought he'd left her safely behind in San Francisco, but here she was at Dianne and Jerome's and so close to him.

When he finally decided to give up and get up for the day, he had a cold shower to wake himself up and try to shake the remnants of his dreams about Pearl. His thoughts about taking her in his arms and showing her how much he missed her.

How much he wanted her.

How much he needed her.

You need to get a grip.

He shook his head and headed downstairs to

get a cup of coffee. The moment he hit the landing, he could hear Derek laughing. He glanced over the banister and saw that Derek was sitting with Pearl on the large sectional couch, in front of the fireplace.

It made his heart skip a beat.

Derek was curled up beside Pearl and she was so cozy with him. She looked happy as Derek was building a three-dimensional puzzle of the Empire State Building.

It looked totally natural for Pearl and Derek to be sitting on the couch together, building a puzzle, and Calum couldn't help but think of the child they'd lost.

"I'm totally freaked out, Calum. How are you not more freaked out?" Pearl had demanded.

"I am freaked out," he said, but really he couldn't stop smiling.

"You don't look freaked out." She ran her hands through her hair. "I can't be a mother!"

"Why not?" he asked.

"I don't know anything about kids or babies or anything. I mean, I guess I could treat a sick child or a baby, but... I'm not the maternal kind of person."

He held her close. "You totally can be."

"My mother is insane."

"I hardly think she's insane."

Pearl laughed nervously. "Okay, but...this is not what I wanted."

"I'm okay with whatever decision you decide, but I'll help you. I'm here and I'm sure we can do this together."

"I think so, too," she whispered. "Still, I'm not sure I'll be the best mother."

"You'll be great."

And it was clear from the way that Pearl was with Derek that she would've been great. It made him sad to think that they didn't have a chance to experience it with their own child. He never had a chance to prove that his instincts about Pearl were right.

Their baby would be around the same age as Derek and he couldn't help but ponder what their child would have been like. He often thought about that when he saw Derek, but he tried not to think about it too much.

Don't think about it.

He had almost had everything he wanted, and then it was taken away. And what did he know about having a family? He didn't have any kind of home life growing up. How could he be a good father?

All his life he had worked hard to get his father's attention and it had gotten him nowhere.

He had no role models and that's what got him through his grief.

That he would never be a good father and maybe it was for the best.

Was it?

He came down the rest of the way and side-stepped the living area, where Derek was busy with Pearl, and headed straight for the kitchen, where Jerome was leaning over the island, holding a cup of coffee.

"Where's Dianne?" Calum asked, pulling down a mug and helping himself to coffee.

"She had to run into town. There was a landslide last night—there's been so much rain in the foothills and they called in everyone they could. She should be back soon."

"You look exhausted," Calum said, taking a sip of coffee.

"Look who's talking," Jerome remarked.

Calum snorted in response. "I tossed and turned all night, but I didn't hear Dianne leave."

"She left about three."

"Do you think the hospital needs help?" Calum asked. He wouldn't mind driving into town and helping out.

"No, Dianne texted about ten minutes ago and she'll be home in a couple of hours. You know, we may be smaller than San Francisco, but we do have coldhearted surgeons out here."

Calum laughed. "Really? I had no idea."

"Smart-ass," Jerome mumbled.

Calum finished his coffee and then headed outside. He needed to take a walk, but when he stepped outside there was a thick layer of fog and it was misting. He didn't really feel like getting soaked if it started to rain, and the temperature had dropped.

So he took a seat in a chair under the covered deck.

"Hey, I thought I saw that you were up."

He looked over his shoulder and saw Pearl standing in the doorway. She pulled the door closed and stepped outside. She had an oversize sweater and a wrap on, but was barefoot as she padded across the deck and took a seat beside him.

"Aren't you cold?" he asked, staring at her feet.

"No. It's warmer here than New York." She

tucked her feet up under her. "I was hoping to go for a walk."

"Me, too, but I don't fancy getting caught in a cold November rain."

"It's not November," she stated. "And it's warm."

"I know, but I don't know a song about rain in the autumn other than that one."

She grinned and her eyes lit up. "I loved that song."

"I remember. It's also one of the songs you like to sing when you've imbibed too much. The rubber chicken would sing it better."

She groaned and buried her head in her hand. "You're never going to let me live that down, are you?"

"Probably not." He then proceeded to yowl, in a really bad impression of her that got her laughing.

"I do not sound that bad."

"I'm afraid you do. You're an excellent surgeon, but a terrible singer."

"You're not that great yourself. And you're a terrible dancer. You have no rhythm."

"What're you talking about?" He got up and

started dancing, which made her reach over and hit him.

"Stop that! You'll scare Derek." Then she pulled out her phone, which was buzzing, and frowned when she saw it. "Oh, no."

"What's wrong?" Calum asked.

"It's George. I know Dianne didn't want me talking about work, that it's supposed to be a holiday, but George isn't tolerating the chemotherapy well. His mother is texting me." Pearl texted George's worried mother back.

"Tell her I'll call the oncologist, we'll do a blood draw and I'll get his dosage changed."

Pearl nodded and Calum pulled out his phone and sent a message to the oncology team at the hospital. His oncologist, as if expecting this, already had done the blood draw. Calum went over the lab report and sent a message back about how to proceed.

Their oncology team was one of the best in San Francisco, but there was a certain procedure to the treatment plan that he'd developed and Calum was the one that had to do the adjustments.

"There, that should help George," Calum said, finishing up his text. "The oncology team is going to keep me posted, but you can tell George's mother that we'll get it under control."

Truth be told it, was worrying him that George wasn't handling the protocol well, but he wasn't going to say that out loud and he didn't really need to—he could see the worry in Pearl's face.

"So Dianne told me that you've helped build this house," Pearl said, changing the subject.

"Yeah, I found I like renovating. My place in San Francisco is an old Victorian home, but she was pretty much condemned when I bought her. I've been slowly fixing it up. Most of the house is inhabitable, but I have a small apartment in the top of the house where I live comfortably."

"What're you going to do with it when it's done?" she asked. "Are you going to stay there or flip it?"

"I don't know. I like living near the hospital, but I also like it out here. I really enjoyed my time here with Jerome as we worked on this place. Still, I like where I work, and I took over Dr. Chin's practice. I'm not sure I could give it all up to move out here."

And, really, who did he have to give it all up for?

No one.

"It's beautiful out here," Pearl said. "I've always loved log cabins and the forest, but my parents aren't exactly nature lovers."

"You don't say?" he teased.

"My dad thinks he's rustic living on a big piece of land that overlooks Puget Sound. He has some trees, but the house is a modern eyesore in the middle of nature and he's never there, but he has a new wife and they have a couple of kids."

"I didn't know that you had half siblings."

"I do, but I'm not really welcome."

"Then why do your parents argue over who you're going to visit every holiday?" he asked.

"My father does it to annoy my mother and for control. He likes to be in control and he likes all the attention on him. That's the only reason. My father's new wife doesn't like me and, trust me, the feeling is mutual."

"So they both fight over you, a grown woman, in order to make each other miserable."

"You got it," she said.

"That's messed up."

Pearl laughed. "You have no idea."

"I think I have an idea. You are aware who my father is, right?"

"I am aware and that is true." She stood up.

"Looks like the rain and the fog is letting up. I think I'm going to go for a walk, after all."

"Would you mind some company?"

What're you doing? That's not keeping away from her.

"Sure."

"All right, I'll grab my jacket and we'll take a hike through the woods. I know where all the trails are."

They got their jackets and Pearl's shoes and headed outside, leaving Derek and Jerome behind to watch cartoons. Derek was excited about going to Mountain View's Founder's Day parade that evening, though Pearl did not share his excitement.

She really detested parades, but it was nice hanging out with Derek.

If her baby had survived, she'd probably be taking him or her out to different holiday parades and just the thought of never being able to experience that made her sad.

Don't think about it.

She didn't want to get lost in those kind of thoughts. Not today. She was just trying to make it through this weekend without things being too weird.

She knew that she probably shouldn't be going on this walk with Calum, but it would be nice to have company, especially company that knew their way around Dianne and Jerome's property. Calum was waiting out front for her. He was wearing a leather jacket and hiking boots. She was glad that she had brought a pair of boots, too. Her sneakers or heels weren't going to cut it in the woods.

"You ready?" he asked.

"As ready as I'll ever be. Hopefully this hike isn't up the side of a mountain or anything."

"Hardly. It's easy, I promise. And besides, you're used to climbing mountains in heels in San Francisco."

"True."

They fell into step and Calum led her down the drive, where there was a small dirt trail off the driveway that disappeared into the woods. She hadn't noticed it last night because it had been too dark, but it looked like a fairly easy, groomed trail and was wide enough for a horse.

"Don't tell me Dianne goes horseback riding?" she asked.

"No, but she lets other riders from around the area use her trail system, so you might have to watch for horse patties."

"Fun." And she really hoped she didn't find a present from a horse.

It was a beautiful day and the sun was starting to come out and melt the last remnants of the fog and mist.

It was nice to walk with Calum. It felt so right. She wished that she could hold on to this. She still wanted him. She loved being with him, here.

Even after all this time.

When he reached out and took her hand, touched her face, it had reignited something deep inside her. Something she thought was long gone, but she'd been kidding herself to think that it was gone. It would never be gone. Not where Calum was concerned.

"About last night," she said, stopping.

He paused. "What about last night?"

"You asked me if I wanted to marry you when I was…" She trailed off, because she couldn't even bring herself to say that she was pregnant once. It was hard to even admit something so painful. "The answer is…yes. I wanted to marry you."

His expression softened and he took a step closer to her. "You did?"

"Well, I didn't want to marry anyone ever, but... I wanted you, Calum."

And she still did.

She still wanted him. She still loved him. Even after all this time. Even though she wasn't really sure what love was.

He didn't respond to that. Instead he closed the gap between them. His hands were in her hair and she was pulled into a deep kiss. The moment his lips touched hers, it ignited that burning passion that was always simmering below the surface.

Her body remembered him and she pressed herself against him, holding on to him, afraid to let him go. This time she didn't want to run.

She was so enraptured by the kiss, his lips against hers, hungrily claiming her, that even the ground was shaking beneath her feet.

Wait. The ground is shaking.

Calum broke off the kiss and held her tight. "It's a quake."

"Right."

Calum held her—there was nowhere for them to go in that moment. They just stood there, on ground that suddenly didn't feel so solid. It felt like they were standing on a big bowl of Jell-O, but as quickly as the shaking started, it was over.

Calum let go of his hold on her and they just stared at each. She was not really expecting the earth to move quite that much.

"That wasn't too bad. I just hope it's not a fore-shock," Calum said, but she could hear that his voice was shaking.

"I forgot about earthquakes and I hope it's not a foreshock, either." Pearl couldn't look at him. She was embarrassed she had let down her guard, but also, she was still a bit rattled by the quake.

"We'd better get back and see if Jerome and Derek are okay."

"Right," she said nervously.

He took her hand without thinking and they walked quickly off the trail and back up to the house. Everything seemed to be fine, but Jerome was standing on his deck holding Derek, who looked a bit shaken, too.

"Thank God. I was worried about you two," Jerome said, setting down Derek, who still stuck close to his father.

"We're okay," Calum said.

"I turned on the police scanner. There doesn't seem to be too much damage yet and Dianne texted that she's on her way home."

"Can I go back inside, Dad?" Derek asked.

Jerome nodded and Derek ran back into the house.

"We were wondering if it was a foreshock. It was strong, but didn't feel that deep like a real quake," Pearl said. She had grown up in California and was used to some real doozy earthquakes.

"Let's hope not. Let's hope it was just a tremor," Calum said.

"Fingers crossed," Jerome said.

It was then a car came up the drive and Jerome let out a sigh when they saw it was Dianne's car. Pearl felt a surge of relief, too.

Jerome greeted his wife and they hugged and kissed. Pearl was envious and she couldn't help but think about the kiss in the forest with Calum. It had come out of nowhere and though she shouldn't have let it happen, because they were only supposed to be friends, she had wanted it, too.

In fact, she wanted more, and it terrified her. It thrilled her, but scared her, too, how much she still wanted him. How she lost all control around him. She pulled back her hand, realizing that she was still holding his hand. He looked at her.

"You okay?" he whispered.

"I'm fine."

"Look, about what happened…"

She shook her head. "You don't have to explain anything else. I'm okay. It's all good and we don't have to talk about it anymore."

A strange expression crossed his face. "Right. We don't have to talk about it."

And he walked away, up the stairs into the house, and Pearl sighed.

When was she ever going to learn?

Just as Pearl expected, the nighttime Founder's Day parade in Mountain View was crowded and she hated it, but what she liked was seeing Derek's excitement and she liked watching Calum with Derek.

He had Derek on his shoulders most of the night and they were laughing and following the parade, with Dianne and Jerome.

Calum was so good with Derek and she couldn't help but wonder what he would've been like with their own child. A lump formed in her throat as she thought about it. About how her life could've been so different.

So much better.

She also couldn't stop thinking about that kiss. Even after the parade ended and they all went back to the ranch. She just couldn't stop thinking about how good it was to be in his arms. How his lips felt against hers. The way he made her blood heat with need. She loved when he held her. When he kissed her. Calum made her feel safe when his arms were around her and how she wanted to be there again, even if just for a night.

They never had their breakup sex.

Can you really just have one night with Calum?

And she knew she couldn't. So it was good that it was just one kiss and they didn't have to talk about it again.

Only she had to stop worrying and thinking about Calum, because when she woke up the next morning it was all hands to the kitchen to prep for a big Founder's Day dinner. It seemed to be a weekend affair in Mountain View. Dianne's parents were driving in, so there would be seven people for dinner and Dianne was not the niftiest in the kitchen.

Not that Pearl was, either.

She was on the sweet-potato-pie duty, which meant mashing the sweet potatoes and adding the most important ingredient—the mini marshmallows—and she took her job seriously.

"You're doing that awfully slow," Calum teased as he was mixing something in a bowl.

"It's got to be just right."

"Just dump them on," he said.

Pearl picked up a mini marshmallow and threw it at him. "Just stick to your assigned tasks."

"I am," he teased, continuing to mix whatever was in the bowl.

"What're you making?" she asked, wrinkling her nose, because whatever was in the bowl smelled awful.

"I think it's pastry, but it doesn't smell right." Calum frowned. "I think I did something wrong. I thought pastry was supposed to be like dough, not like…"

"It looks like wallpaper paste. You better go back to the drawing board on that one."

He winced. "Well, you need to move faster or that sweet-potato pie will never get done."

She tossed another marshmallow at him as he retreated to the other side of the kitchen. She wanted to make sure that everything looked

okay. Jerome was outside barbecuing the turkey, or smoking it—Pearl couldn't really tell. She
continued placing marshmallows on the sweet-
potato pie. She wasn't the best cook, so she really hoped she didn't make someone sick and
that the pie tasted good.

There was a rumble and she froze. "What was
that?"

"What was what?" Calum asked as he bent
over a recipe book.

And then the rumble came again—this time
there was clattering of dishes and then the big
shake came.

"Oh, my God." She froze, terrified.

Calum was beside her in a second and grabbed
her, dragging her under a door frame. They
braced themselves as the house heaved. This was
more than just the tremor that they experienced
when they were in the woods.

This was the real deal. She was hoping that
the previous tremor was just that—a tremor—
and not a prelude to what was happening now.
Even though she grew up in California, she could
never get used to the quakes and still remembered the big quake in San Francisco.

Calum's arms were around her and she felt

safe. She snuggled closer, holding on to him as the floor beneath them shook. She buried her head against his shoulder.

It felt like it went on for an eternity, but it ended. Her pulse was thundering and she still clung to him. It felt right to hold him and to be held by him.

"Pearl," he whispered. "Are you okay? I didn't mean to grab you so forcefully."

"I'm okay and that's fine. I'm glad you did."

Of course, it was a bit of a fib. She wasn't okay and she didn't want to let go of her hold on Calum. She just clung to him as if he was her safety net and though she never really wanted to ever rely on someone, she liked being here with him. His arms were so strong and she had never felt this safe before. His arms were tight around her, holding her close, and she closed her eyes as she listened to his heart.

She could stay here forever.

"Derek!"

The blood-curdling scream from Dianne sent a chill down her spine and she was off running outside. She'd forgotten that Jerome, Dianne and Derek were outside when the earthquake hit.

Calum was behind her and they couldn't see any of them.

The barbecue was on its side, the turkey on the ground.

Calum shut off the gas line with a wrench from the meter that ran alongside the pipe outside.

"Dianne?" Pearl shouted.

Jerome came running around the corner of the house—he was bleeding. "This way!"

Pearl and Calum followed him around to the side of the barn, and back behind the barn they found Dianne crouched beside rubble, and it looked like a piece of the barn had collapsed. Pearl's stomach twisted in a knot as she got closer and saw it wasn't only rubble that Dianne was crouched beside.

She saw a small arm from underneath.

It was Derek.

He was trapped.

CHAPTER NINE

THE AMBULANCE WAS on the way and Calum was
thankful that Pearl had her phone on her. He
helped Jerome move the rubble away as Pearl
held Dianne.

As soon as they got visualization and Calum
knew it was safe, he got beside Derek and as-
sessed his ABCs without trying to disturb him.
If there was a crush injury, a spinal injury, he
didn't want to move Derek, who was bent over a
barrel. Calum was really worried that there was
damage to Derek's spine, as the barn collapsing
had stretched him in an odd way over the side
of the barrel.

A curl of dread uncoiled in the pit of his stomach and he hoped Derek would come through
this. He'd known Derek the boy's whole life. He
was terrified, seeing Derek there, but he com-
partmentalized it and got to work. He wouldn't
let Derek die.

Jerome, even though he was a doctor, tried to take Derek's hand, but Calum stilled him.

"Don't move him. Not until we get a backboard. There could be damage to his spine."

"Oh, God," Jerome said.

"It's okay. I've got this. Get the paramedics here and send Pearl over."

Jerome nodded and left.

Pearl crouched down beside Calum.

"Derek," she whispered, her voice shaking.

"I'm worried about his spine," Calum said. "See how he's bent."

Pearl craned her neck. "Yes. We can get him on a backboard and get him to the hospital."

"We're going to the hospital," Calum stated. "I'm not letting just anyone touch his spine and I need you in there with me."

Pearl nodded and he could see that glint of determination in her eyes. He only wanted her by his side when he operated on Derek. Together, they could save Derek's life. He was certain of that.

"Of course. I agree, we should be the only surgeons working on him."

Pearl stood to let in the paramedics. Calum directed them with easing Derek to the backboard, not shaking Derek and protecting the spine. Once Calum felt he was secure, he let the paramedics do the rest of their work, to make sure Derek was stabilized.

"Calum," Dianne said, tears running down her face as she clung to Jerome.

"He's breathing. I'm going with the paramedics to the hospital and I'm going to make sure that I'm consulted if there's a single bone broken."

"I'm going, too," Pearl stated.

Dianne nodded. "We'll follow."

Calum stood by Derek's side and helped the paramedics wheel the stretcher back to the ambulance. Pearl was on the other side and they climbed into the back of the ambulance after Derek was loaded.

Calum's pulse was racing. He was so worried about the little broken human in front of him, and he prayed that the spinal cord wasn't severed; that he could save Derek from paralysis. He looked up at Pearl and she met his gaze.

She didn't smile, but he could see the concern in her eyes, too.

He could see her worry and pain as the ambulance raced down the hill, down into town.

"It'll be tricky," one of the paramedics said.

"There are power lines down and trees. The hospital is bombarded after the quake."

"We're both surgeons from San Francisco and we'll help any way we can, but after we make sure Derek is okay."

The paramedic nodded.

There wasn't much to say. He'd work for days on end, straight, if it meant he could use hospital privileges and save Derek's life. He would've done the same for his own child.

He would do the same for Pearl.

Once they got to the hospital, there was mass confusion in the emergency department, but he had to focus on Derek.

"What do we have here?" a trauma doctor asked, meeting them at the door.

"Male, age five, suspected break to the spine. GCS score in the field was five, but improved upon arrival to nine," the paramedic stated.

"And who are you?" the trauma doctor asked, looking at the both of them. "Are you the parents?"

"No. I'm Dr. Munro, orthopedic surgeon, and this is Dr. Henderson, also an orthopedic surgeon, and we'll be leading this case."

"This is my ER," the trauma doctor shouted.

"And we're specialists in spines," Pearl snapped. "The parents will be arriving soon and have given us permission to take care of their son. This is Dr. Dianne Lopez's child."

The trauma surgeon nodded. "You can use trauma pod three. We're slammed."

"I promise, we'll help you after we make sure that Derek is stable," Calum offered. He hadn't asked Pearl if she was willing to help, but he knew that she would. She might shirk other duties, but she never shirked her medical duties.

The patient always came first.

The paramedics wheeled Derek into trauma pod three and the trauma team helped Calum get into a yellow trauma gown.

"I'll go speak with the chief of surgery," Pearl said, tying the back of her gown.

"Okay, he may have a break in his spine. We need to move him carefully, make sure he's stable and then I need a CT scan stat. We could be looking at crush injuries." Calum helped the team move Derek's backboard onto the bed so the paramedics could have back their stretcher.

Calum leaned over Derek and checked the vitals again.

There was reaction to the pupils, so he had

hope that there wasn't a head trauma and that Derek wasn't bleeding in his brain.

Pearl returned. "Shall we get him down to the CT? We have clearance. The chief was very accommodating."

"Yes. He's breathing, intubated, but he's as stable as he's going to be and we need to find out what's going on in there."

Pearl nodded and they worked together to make sure that all the lines and all the bags were secured. Then they wheeled him out of the trauma pod, following one of the nurses to where the MRI was and where they jumped the line.

Together, Pearl and Calum lifted the backboard and secured Derek so that he was able to have his scans.

He had to drag Pearl away into the other room so they could do the scan. Truth be told, he had to drag himself away. It was hard to leave Derek alone and vulnerable, even though the child wasn't aware what was going on.

The radiologist had come down so that he could interpret the scans, but Calum had seen enough scans to know what he was looking for. Pearl worried her lip, her arms crossed, and kept her eyes on Derek.

"He's so little," she whispered.

"I know."

"This shouldn't have happened to him."

"I know."

She glanced at him—there were tears in her eyes, and he'd never seen her like this before. So close to crying. "I can do this, it's just…when you have a moment to feel…"

Calum sighed. "I know."

"I'm scared, Calum. Scared for Derek."

He took her in his arms and held her. She clung to him and he held her close while they waited for the scans to come up.

"Scans are up, Dr. Munro," the radiologist, Dr. Redding, said.

He let go of her then.

Calum leaned over and winced when he saw that there was a fracture, but the cord appeared to be intact. Derek was going to need a fusion. There were a couple of ribs that were broken, but they were hairline fractures and didn't appear to be infiltrating his lungs.

"There appears to be a bit of internal bleeding near the spleen, but it doesn't appear to be excessive and is quite normal for a crush injury.

We can monitor it and see if it gets any worse," Dr. Redding said.

"Thank you, Dr. Redding." Calum turned to Pearl. "We need to get him into the OR and we need to know where to go."

Pearl nodded. "You stay with Derek and I'll fill in Dianne and Jerome what's happening and speak to the chief of surgery again. We'll have him in the operating room as soon as possible, I'm sure."

"Thank you."

Pearl nodded. "Just keep our boy stable."

It stunned him when she said that. *Our* boy. He wasn't their boy, but it felt like he could've been. Their child would've been the same age.

Derek swallowed a lump that had formed in his throat. He had to be strong, he had to clear his head to be able to do this.

He was going to make sure Derek was taken care of. He wasn't going to let down Derek, Dianne or Jerome.

Pearl looked down through her microscope at the spinal cord of her godson. Really, they shouldn't be working on him, but there were no specialists like them in this hospital. They were Derek's only chance.

Dianne and Jerome had given their permission and the chief of surgery graciously was assisting on Derek. They had everything they needed and it was hard to keep Dianne and Jerome out of the operating room.

Especially Dianne, who wanted to do the anesthesiology on her son, but that was against every oath they took. She couldn't work on her son. She couldn't be present in the operating room and Pearl couldn't even imagine the pain of being so helpless.

Can't you?

And just that thought made her recall in vivid detail the absolute agony of losing her baby. Of losing Calum and her baby. How she had felt so helpless and there was nothing she could do to stop it. Her medical degree had been useless in that moment when her baby passed.

It was extreme, agonizing helplessness.

"The T4 and T5 are crushed. We're going to have fuse here and place rods," Calum muttered.

"I agree," Pearl said, hoping that her voice didn't shake.

Calum glanced up at her briefly. "Pearl?"

"I'm okay," she said. "I can do this."

"Good, because I need you," Calum said.

It caught her off guard. She knew that he meant he needed her for this surgery. He needed her expertise and assistance, just like he had needed her when they were working on their patient with skeletal dysplasia. They were a team. Right in this moment they needed each other.

He was staring at her, his blue eyes intense across the operating-room table.

"I need you, too," she said. "We got this."

The corners of his eyes crinkled and she knew that he was smiling under his mask. "Right. We do."

Pearl nodded and went back to work. She was going to make sure that Derek wasn't paralyzed. She was going to take care of Dianne and Jerome's little boy.

This is why she became a surgeon.

You walked away from it, remember?

She found her work rewarding, but there was something different about being in an operating room and working on a patient's spine after an accident compared to a busted knee or a torn rotator cuff after a sports injury.

This was saving a life. The deep-rooted part of

her emotions wanted to run because she wanted to cry seeing Derek like this. She was losing control of herself seeing Derek on this table, but she couldn't run from Derek. Derek needed her. Dianne and Jerome needed her and Calum needed her.

Right here.

Her control over her emotions had to wait and she'd lose control if it meant Derek would be saved. She'd do anything to save him.

This was what she'd been born to do as a surgeon. This was what she missed, and she was angry that she walked away from it, and she wished she could go back.

You can.

Only she wasn't sure that she was strong enough to do that. She wasn't sure that she could turn back the clock and walk back into her old life.

She was too terrified, but she had to try.

Pearl walked with Calum down to the small waiting room. Dianne and Jerome were there, on their own. Pearl saw that Jerome's head had been bandaged and she was glad someone had taken care of his superficial laceration.

She felt bad for ignoring it, but their main focus was Derek.

When they walked in, Dianne's eyes were wide, she was pale, and Jerome put his arm around her. The surgery had taken hours and when Pearl checked the clock, it was six in the morning. They'd been working all night. She was beat.

"He made it through the surgery," Calum said. "We had to fuse his spine. He had a couple of crushed vertebrae. He has a long recovery, but I feel confident that he will walk again."

Dianne started sobbing and then hugged Calum and then her.

"I don't know what would've happened if you two weren't there," Dianne sobbed.

Tears were stinging Pearl's eyes. "Well, we were, and Derek is stable. He's going to be okay, but he's in the intensive-care unit. He's under the care of the paediatric surgeon on duty."

"And that surgeon has my pager if something else happens," Calum said. "I will be here in a heartbeat."

Dianne hugged him. "Thank you. Thank you both. Can we go see him?"

"I don't think the ICU doctor on duty is going

to stop Dr. Lopez from seeing her son," Pearl teased.

Dianne nodded and left with Jerome.

Pearl sighed. "So much for a relaxing weekend, huh?"

Calum chuckled and sank down in a chair, scrubbing his hand over his face. "What a day."

"Not exactly how I thought it would go." She sat down in the chair next to him. "I was going to take an early morning train to get back to San Francisco. I missed it."

"I'll take you home. I drove here and it'll be faster than the train."

"Thanks. I appreciate that."

"Well, if I had known that you were coming to the ranch I could have driven you here."

Pearl cocked an eyebrow. "Would you? Especially with how things were a bit awkward before we came?"

"Okay, maybe not when I was in that frame of mind. You're right, but I can give you a ride back to San Francisco today. I just need some strong, strong coffee and then we can head back. I haven't checked the extent of the damage from the quake."

"We've been busy." Pearl stood up. "I think

we'd better check with the chief of surgery and make sure that we're not needed, as we did promise to help out if we got privileges."

Calum yawned. "Right."

"Come on. You can do a few more hours' work and we'll head back."

"Point me in the direction of caffeine and I can spend some time setting bones or putting shoulders back into place."

"That's the spirit."

They left the waiting room. She was completely and utterly exhausted. Not just physically, but emotionally just done.

She was burnt out. Burnt out from all the emotions that she was trying so hard to control, burnt out from trying to keep everyone out, but she didn't know how to go back.

There was no way to turn back time, but she knew one thing—she had to figure out how to get back. She was tired of running.

CHAPTER TEN

"I'M SORRY, BUT the road is closed."

Pearl groaned inwardly as the state trooper talked to Calum. They had left Dianne and Jerome's ranch. Dianne's parents had got in and were updated on the situation. They were going to take shifts going to the hospital.

Pearl helped Dianne's mother clean up what they could and make sure that there was food and everything was okay. Then she packed up her bags. They had hit the road back to San Francisco in the late afternoon. Both of them were wiped out and now there was a washout from the rainstorm that had picked up.

They were stuck and they were too tired to drive back up into the foothills two hours behind them and they were too tired to try and find a detour to get to San Francisco. They were stuck.

"Do you know of any hotels around here?" Calum asked the trooper. Things seemed to be conspiring against them to get back to San Francisco.

"Sure. About three miles back into Catfish Canyon, there's a small motel that would be able to accommodate you. Follow this road back, take the first exit into town and follow Main Street until you find the Golden Corral Motel."

"Thank you, officer."

The state trooper stepped back and Calum did a U-turn and headed back into the last small town they had blasted through on their way back to San Francisco.

She didn't really want to stop for the night, especially with Calum, but at least at a motel she could get her own room. They had used their exhaustion as an excuse not to talk about what happened the day in the woods, or how she had clung to him during the quake.

Or the fact that in the surgery he had said that he always wanted her and she had admitted to the same. It wasn't a lie. She missed him.

She wanted him and she wanted to talk to him. She was overwhelmed and Calum made her feel safe.

It was no problem finding the motel, and despite its name, it actually looked kind of cute and cheerful, which was hard to pull off in a downpour. Calum ran inside to see if there were any rooms.

Pearl hoped there were, because she was exhausted. She wanted a hot shower and bed.

And Calum?

She shook away that thought.

Yes. She wanted Calum again, but there was no way she was going to let that happen. Although, she couldn't get that kiss out of her head. It's all she could think about. It wasn't long before he came back to the car.

"Were there any rooms?" she asked.

"Yes. There was one."

She raised her eyebrows. "One?"

"Yes. So I took it."

"Calum!"

"Pearl, we're adults and we're both tired. I think we can share a room. It has a queen-size bed and a pullout couch. I think we can make do."

She sighed. It wasn't ideal, especially when she needed to put space between the two of them. Not that she was expecting him to do anything—she was worried about hurting him, about not being able to resist him. She was worried that she would want his kisses again, to be held by him. She was worried about how much she wanted it.

"Come on. We can't sit here in the car all night."

"You're right." She reached into the back and grabbed her suitcase, and Calum grabbed his bag. They ran to their room and Calum opened the door.

It was a clean room and there was a sofa bed, a queen bed, a tiny kitchenette and a tiny bathroom. It wasn't perfect, but it would do for one night and she could manage that.

"You take the bed and I'm good on the pullout."

"I can sleep on the pullout," she said. "You've been driving and—"

"What kind of gentleman would I be if I didn't let you have the bed?"

She blushed. "Okay, but no complaining about a bad back tomorrow."

"I don't have a bad back. I slept on these all the time when I was in college."

"That was a very long time ago," she teased.

"Ha, ha." There was a twinkle in his eye. "Do you want a shower first or should I?"

"You go first, since I'm getting the better bed

and I'll see if I can order in some pizza or something."

"Sounds good."

Pearl kicked off her shoes and sat down on the bed, which was surprisingly comfortable, and flipped open the book with all the amenities while Calum grabbed his bag and headed into the bathroom.

It wasn't long before she could hear the water running and she tried not to think about the fact that he was in there, naked.

You need to order pizza and not fantasize about your ex-fiancé who is in the shower.

She found what looked like a good pizza place and ordered a pepperoni pizza. Once she'd finished ordering, Calum came out of the bathroom, only wrapped in a towel. She tried not to stare at him.

"You'd better get dressed," she said.

"I will."

"The pizza guy will be here soon and I'm going to have my shower."

"Once you go in for your shower, I'll get dressed."

Pearl left the money for the pizza on the bed and then grabbed what she needed for a shower, including a change of clothes. She wasn't coming out in a skimpy motel towel. It was bad enough that Calum had.

When her shower was done and she was dressed in a fresh set of comfy clothes, she left the bathroom and hoped that Calum had gotten dressed. She was relieved to see that he had and that the pizza had arrived.

"You came out just in time," Calum said. "It just got here."

"Good. I'm starving. I was hoping for a Founder's Day dinner or some leftovers, but the earthquake had had something else in mind." She put away her stuff and walked over to the kitchenette and took a seat at the little table, hoping her towel holding her wet hair up didn't slip over her face.

"I was watching the television and the earthquake's epicenter was in the Sierra mountain range. We weren't far from it."

"I can believe that. Was there much damage?"

"Yes, and a few deaths."

"We're lucky Derek wasn't one of them."

"I know," he said. "I got an update from Dr. Knowles, the paediatrician attending, and Derek is doing well. He's still in the ICU, but they're thinking of waking him soon from his medicated coma. He's stable and there have been motor responses from his lower limbs."

Pearl sighed in relief. "Thank goodness."

"Do you ever think about our child?"

The question caught her off guard. Of course she did. All the time, but she tried not to. Work kept her busy, kept her distracted, so that she didn't have to think about their baby. And the fact that the question came from Calum shocked her.

She couldn't think about it when she ran off to New York. It was a foolish thing to do, but Pearl realized that when it came to matters of the heart, when it came close to her fear of losing something she wanted so badly, she fled.

It was easier to manage that pain.

"I do," she said quietly. "I do all the time."

"I'm surprised."

"Why would you be surprised by that?"

"Because you left, because I tried to talk to you about it and you left," he said.

"I left because I... Because I failed, Calum. I failed you. I failed our child. I'm the reason the baby was lost. My incompetent cervix. I failed you." She couldn't stop the tears then and she couldn't believe that she had let that out. She'd never cried in front of him before and there was no way she could stop them now.

She was struggling to accept that she had told him; that she was vulnerable to him.

She was never vulnerable to anyone. She'd been taught that vulnerability was a weakness, by both her parents, but she couldn't hold it back anymore. She was tired keeping everything in, and she wasn't less of a person for feeling something.

"You didn't fail me. Your body failed us, but not really. Why didn't you tell me this before?"

Tears slid down her cheeks and the dam burst. There was no more holding back. "I shouldn't be crying."

"Why?"

"I was told tears were a weakness. Tears meant failure, and failure was a weakness. You think I'm a strong person, cold and detached, but I'm not. I'm not."

"You're the strongest person I know, Pearl."

Calum couldn't believe she was crying. That she blamed herself.

He knew that's why the baby had been lost,

but not that she carried the blame. She thought she'd let him down.

He didn't feel that she had let him down because she lost the baby; she'd let him down because she left. But now she was crying and he hated to see her cry.

When he'd held her in his arms during the earthquake, he had wanted to keep her there. He had wanted to comfort her, because she had never let him comfort her before. Even when they were together, there had always been barriers between them. She had never let him in.

He closed the gap between them and took her in his arms. Tipping her chin, he kissed her on the lips, wanting her to know he didn't blame her for the loss of their child, but he was unable to say that he was still hurt she had left him.

All he wanted to do was hold her, to kiss her and just be with her. Even if it was only one more time. He just wanted her. He'd always wanted her.

"Calum," she murmured against his lips.

"Pearl, I've missed you."

Her lips were so soft, he wanted to savor them. He so wanted to savor every second with her. He wanted her so badly.

He broke the kiss and stepped away, unsure of what to do. Unsure of everything. Pearl was standing so close to him. Just a few feet away. That's all that separated them. Maybe that's all that ever had. Maybe they were closer than he thought.

"Calum?" she asked, and her breath hitched. Her face was flush with desire and her eyes were still moist with tears.

Their first time together they'd been intoxicated. This time the only thing impeding him was his heart and the only thing he was drunk on was her.

Only her.

It had always been only her.

"I want you, Pearl. I've always wanted you."

"I meant what I said in that operating room, Calum. I've only ever wanted you, too."

Then why did you leave?

Only he didn't say that out loud. He just stared at her, his pulse thundering in his ears, his blood burning with need to have her again. To never let her go.

"You really mean that?" he asked.

"I want tonight, Calum. I want you. Please. Even if it's just for one night."

There was no other answer needed. He closed the gap between them, reaching down to cup her face and kiss her again. Gently at first and then possessively, letting her know how much he wanted her. How much he only wanted her.

There had never been a time when he hadn't wanted her. There would never be time when he wouldn't desire her. Pearl was everywhere. She was in every dream, every memory of the best times of his life. She was like a ghost haunting him. She was everything.

Pearl melted under his lips, her arms around his neck and her fingers tangling in the hair at the nape. He pushed her over to the bed. He knew he shouldn't, but he missed her, and she wanted it as much as he did.

Calum wanted to chase away the memories of their loss, her leaving, by making love to her. Even if it was just for one night.

"Are you sure, Pearl?" he asked again. "I don't have protection."

"I'm sure," she murmured against his ear. "I'm on the pill. It's okay."

"Pearl…"

She silenced him with a kiss, then undid his

belt. "I want you, Calum. I've always wanted you."

The moment her hands slipped under the waist of his jeans, he moaned. He knew he was a lost man and he had to have her.

"You're all I've ever wanted, Pearl." He cupped her breasts and kissed that spot below her collarbone that he remembered so well. She moaned with pleasure. This is what he'd been dreaming of since she'd left.

Calum lowered her to the mattress, running his hands over her body, but pressing himself against her so he could feel her against him, feel every inch of her. He desperately wanted to be skin-to-skin.

Nothing separating them.

"Touch me," she whispered, wrapping her legs around his waist.

"Pearl, you're driving me crazy."

"I don't care. I want you. Now."

Her urgency really drove him wild with desire.

With hurried fingers they undressed so that nothing was between them. She ran her hand over his skin, causing gooseflesh to break out. He loved the softness of her touch.

"Yes. Touch me," he said.

"With pleasure." She teased him with the tips of her fingers, running a finger lightly down his chest, over his nipples, along his ribs, lower and lower until she gripped him in the palm of her hand, stroking him.

"Oh, God," he groaned.

"I love it when you moan," she said huskily, still holding him. She leaned forward to kiss his neck, and her eyes were glittering the darkness of the room as she continued to stroke him, holding him captive to her touch.

Every nerve was burning under her touch. It was driving him wild. He didn't want her to stop, but he didn't want to come. Not this way, but it felt so good.

"Don't stop."

"I don't plan on it." And then her kisses trailed down his body until her mouth was on him, then his hand slipped into her hair. He wanted to be inside her, bring her pleasure.

The same pleasure she was giving him.

Growling, he pulled her away and then pushed her back against the mattress. She wrapped her legs around him and he moved them, pulling her legs open.

"Calum, I want you."

"I know, but now it's my time. I want to taste you."

"Your turn…oh, my God." She cried out as he did exactly what he said he would do. He was using his tongue to taste her, running his tongue around the most sensitive part of her, making her thighs quiver as he brought her close to the edge of ecstasy. Just like she had done to him.

"Calum!" she cried out.

"What?" he asked, knowing what she wanted. He wanted it, too. Badly.

He just wanted her to beg for it. To ask for it.

"You know."

"No, I don't." And he went back to his ministrations, her hands in his hair, her back arched.

"Calum!"

"Tell me what you want, Pearl. Tell me."

"I want you."

He moved over her and entered her with one quick thrust.

Oh, God.

She was so tight, so hot, and it took every ounce of control he had not to take her hard and fast, like his body was screaming for him to do. He wanted to make this last.

He wanted to savor this moment, if it was to only be one night.

He wanted this one night to last forever.

Only he knew that it wouldn't.

So he thrust slowly, agonizingly so, making her cry out, and he didn't have long to wait. She began to meet his thrusts, urging him to go faster. They moved in sync like no time had passed between them, like they had done this so many times before. Like it was yesterday. He sank deeper, lost to her. He held her tight, his hand cupping her bottom as he let her ride him.

It was frenzied, fast and hot. It was everything to be that connected with her again and when he thought he couldn't take much more she cried out, tightening around as she came, her nails digging into his back.

Only then did he let go of his control and join her. It had been so long.

Far too long.

He rolled away when it was over, trying to catch his breath and process what had happened. How powerful it had been. How deep their connection was, but there was no trust and there was nothing keeping her here. Just a job and she could leave him again.

They had made no promises to each other.
Don't think about it now.

Only it was hard not to think about right here. She curled up next to him and he put his arm around her. They didn't say anything to each other and he didn't want to say anything. He didn't want to ruin this moment. He just held her, listening to the sound of their breathing and the sound of the rain on the roof.

He wanted her again.

He was lost and he realized that, no matter how much he wanted to deny it.

He would always be lost.

Always.

CHAPTER ELEVEN

One month later, end of November

"I DON'T KNOW how much longer I can go on, Doc."

Pearl worried her lip and looked at George. He didn't look well. The port in his leg that was feeding chemotherapy straight to the tumor was doing a number on him, but Calum had been insistent that they needed to do a month of the targeted chemo to shrink the osteosarcoma before he even thought of operating.

The chemo that Calum's oncologists were using was very potent and George was no longer that robust athlete—he was wasting away to nothing and the first thing on Pearl's mind was that he had an infection.

Calum was sympathetic. "You're almost done. One more session and I'll determine when I can go in and do the surgery. Hang in there."

George nodded and laid back down. He was

now an inpatient. Two days after he'd started the chemotherapy he began to get constant fevers, and since his mom had to travel back and forth, Pearl and his coach had thought it best that he stay in the hospital to be monitored.

Pearl knew that George wanted to go back to Philadelphia for Christmas and it was hard to be stuck in the hospital, even being an adult. George wasn't the only one in the hospital. Poor Derek still was and Pearl wanted to go see him, but George needed her and Mountain View was too far for just a quick visit.

And she was also fighting something. It was hitting her hard today. Some kind of bug she just couldn't shake.

Derek was doing well and there was no paralysis thanks to her and Calum. He was still in the hospital getting physiotherapy, but he was doing brilliantly. Pearl and Calum were planning to go up there and visit soon, but right now they both needed to be in San Francisco with their patients.

They left George's room. Which she was thankful for, because the room was hot. George was always cold.

"You're sweating. Are you okay?" Calum asked.

"Yeah. It was hot in there."

Calum frowned. "Not especially. I hope you're not getting sick."

"I hope not, either." The last thing she needed was a bug. "I'm fighting something, but I don't have a fever. I checked before I went into George's room."

George looked as awful as Pearl felt. And she'd been feeling poorly since the end of October. Just after she and Calum had spent that incredible night together. Their one night. The next day they made it back to San Francisco and agreed that they would go back to being friends and work together. She had been busy traveling with the team and she hadn't seen him or George in a couple of weeks. She wanted to talk to Calum about their night together, but with this sickness and work she hadn't had a chance to talk to him.

It was fine for the first week and then Pearl had caught this bug, probably from the rain and getting wet that night, but she just couldn't shake it. Calum had been inviting her out, but she was just feeling awful.

"You know, you've been feeling run-down for a couple of weeks. Maybe you are getting sick," Calum suggested.

"I can't get sick. If I get sick, then I can't help George. I haven't had a sick day in years! I get my flu shots regularly, I do everything right. The only thing I can think of was it was that night in the motel. We were both soaked to the bone when we got into the room."

Just thinking about that night made her flush with heat.

They had both agreed that was a one-time thing, but there was a part of her that didn't want it to be. Especially while they worked on the case. She had thought that spending one night with Calum would be enough. That it would get him out of her system, but it hadn't.

It made her crave his touch again.

She'd forgotten what it was like to be in his arms. How he made her feel.

No one had ever made her feel the way that Calum did.

It just made her want more and she didn't deserve to have more.

She was glad she had told Calum how she felt about the loss of their baby, and he'd said that he didn't blame her, but she had a hard time believing it. Other than asking her to come out with

him, he didn't seem all that interested in starting anything up.

It hurt her, but she couldn't blame him.

And it was for the best.

"That could've done it. Why don't we do a
blood test and see if you have infection or something?" he asked.

"That's a good idea." She'd been thinking
about doing it herself, but she'd been so drained
of energy that all she was trying to do was keep
it together to get through work. Her patients
needed her.

She didn't have time for this nonsense.

And if she had an infection she couldn't go see
Derek, either.

She followed Calum into a small exam room
and he washed his hands, then pulled out everything needed for a blood draw.

"If I'm sick, you're still going up to see Derek,
right?" she asked.

"Yes. I will," he said. "My father wanted me to
come see him. Said he had something important
to tell me, but honestly I don't really care what
he has to say."

"Are you sure you don't want to hear it? He's

never reached out before. My parents reach out all the time and they have nothing new to tell me."

"That may be so, but he put work before me and my mom. He left her and even though he made all this money, he barely gave her alimony. Mom gave everything she had for me and my sister. So really, there's nothing I have to say to someone who runs away."

That last comment caught her off guard. She didn't think it was directed at her, but she wasn't sure. Isn't that what she'd done? She'd run away.

"I'm sorry for bringing it up."

"It's okay. Now, stop moving for a few moments and I'll do this blood draw."

"Yes." She winced when the needle pricked her. She had a medical degree, but hated needles, especially when they came near her.

"There. All done." Calum pulled out the needle and placed a cotton swab on her arm. "Now apply pressure."

"I know."

He chuckled. "I'll run this down to the lab and put a rush on it. No sense in dallying around if you're sick. Might as well treat it."

"What about George?" she asked.

Calum sighed. "I know. He's going for a repeat

scan so I can see if the cancer has shrunk, but honestly I don't think that the chemo is touching it. I've never done my surgical procedure on someone with such a large tumor. I don't have a lot of faith that he'll play again and if he continues this way, I'm worried that he won't make it."

"Me, too," she sighed.

"We'll worry about that after his scan and then we'll talk to him and his mother about the options. I don't think he'll be happy."

"You mean about amputation?"

"It would save his life."

"Would it, though?" she asked. "His dream has been to play in the NFL—your procedure could save his leg."

"*Could* is the key word, Pearl. *Could*. There's no guarantee. Medicine is not infallible. Things don't always turn out the way you want." He left the exam room and Pearl leaned back against the chair.

Boy, did she ever know that feeling.

She knew that things didn't always turn out the way you wanted. If they did, she'd never have left San Francisco and she'd have a kid Derek's age.

Then another part of her worried whether she'd still be with Calum. Just a small part because her heart still believed it would've worked out. She could've had a happily-ever-after.

Pearl was called down to the CT room and her heart sank when she saw that Calum was sitting next to Dr. Knox and the tension in the room was palpable.

"What's wrong?"

"Come see," Calum said grimly.

Pearl leaned over and her stomach churned. The osteosarcoma wasn't being shrunk by the chemotherapy. It was invading further. It was like the poison that was used to kill cancer was doing nothing.

The radiation that George had endured was doing nothing.

Immunotherapy was doing nothing.

Nothing was working and there was only one option.

"It's a beast," Calum said.

"Oh, God." Tears were welling up in her eyes. "This is going to...devastate him."

And she didn't want to cry in front of Calum and Dr. Knox. Pearl left the CT room and stood in the hall, trying to breathe. What had come over her? What was wrong with her?

She'd had other patients who had had their careers stalled or ended because of cancer or injuries. She'd always managed to keep her emotions in check.

"Pearl?" Calum asked, following her.

"I'm sorry. I don't know what came over me. I know there's no other option."

Calum nodded. "I'm sorry, but he hid his symptoms too long and I get why. My mother did the same. She hid them, ignored them, until it was too late."

Pearl nodded, but she couldn't control her tears. "I don't know what I'm going to tell the owners."

"You're worried about the owners of the Bridgers?" Calum asked sardonically. "You think that you'll lose your job over this?"

"No, I'm worried about George's future," she stated. "They knew it was a long shot, but still… this whole thing. It's going to ruin a lot of his plans, his career in football."

"Well, cancer has a way of doing that."

"I'm sorry. I'm having a hard time explaining what I want to say. It's all a big mess."

"You need to pull yourself together," Calum stated.

She glared at him. "You're being unkind."

"I'm not being unkind. I know you and I know

that you don't like appearing this way. I know that you don't like to lose control."

She sighed. "I can't remember the last time I lost control."

And then it hit her.

Yes, she did remember the last time she was a bundle of nerves. She recalled in vivid detail the last time she'd cried at the drop of a hat. The last time she felt so ill, so sweaty and uncomfortable.

Oh, God.

"Have my lab results come in?" she asked, hoping her voice wasn't shaking.

"I don't know." Calum pulled out his phone and then checked his messages. "Yeah. They have."

He handed her the phone so she could open the file. She glanced through it all, showing normal blood work, except one thing.

One thing that could be detected in the blood but was too early to detect in a urine test and was too early to detect because her period was not yet late.

The hCG in her bloodstream didn't lie.

The lab result didn't lie.

She was pregnant.

Again.

"Pearl, what's wrong?" Calum asked. "You've gone pale. You look like you're going to faint."

She handed him back the phone, because he had the right to know. He was the father, after all. He took the phone from her and went through the report and his eyes widened when he saw what she saw.

"You're pregnant?"

She nodded. "It appears so."

"I thought you were on the pill?"

"I was, but apparently that didn't work. You know that no form of contraception is perfect. We had protection the first time we got pregnant."

Calum scrubbed a hand over his face. "It seems like the fates *want* us to have a baby as we seem to get pregnant in spite of using the proper protection."

"Right?" She laughed nervously.

She didn't know what she was going to do. Her job involved traveling. She sometimes had to leave San Francisco and travel to other states to be there when the team played. And she had offers from other teams who wanted her. Offers she'd been seriously considering so that she could put distance between her and Calum since their night together.

Running away again.

"Well, I think I know the best solution to this whole mess."

Pearl cocked an eyebrow, intrigued. "You do?"

"I think we need to do what we were going to do the first time."

"Are you serious?" she snapped. "You think that's the best course of action? Look what happened last time."

"I know what happened last time," Calum stated quietly. "You lost the baby and left. I distinctly remember what happened last time."

"So if you remember what happened last time, why do think that repeating that mistake is a good idea?"

He took a step back, shocked. "Mistake?"

"We didn't plan it. And we didn't plan this one. Do you really think that marrying me is the best course of action?"

"I do. I think a family should be together. And that's why I want you to marry me."

"Because of duty? That's why you want to marry me. That's the only reason. I can't marry you because of your sense of outdated duty,

Calum. Look how that turned out for my parents and look at your parents. A family can't be forced together."

His expression hardened. "Your parents are hardly a good example."

"Exactly."

"And my parents…" He trailed off. "It wouldn't be like that. We're not like them."

"How do you know?" she asked.

"We're better than them, Pearl."

"Are we? Are we really?" she asked.

"Pearl, I'm asking you. Marry me."

"And I'm saying no, Calum. I can't marry you. Our lives are so different…" She was terrified of losing the baby again, of losing Calum.

She was losing control and she felt like she was going to be sick. She was scared of reaching out and taking her happily-ever-after.

"Right, and you'll leave again if a job comes up. Your career means more to you because for whatever reason you're trying to please parents who will never be pleased with you. Why can't you see that?" He asked that with such anger, it caught her off guard.

"It's my career. And look who's talking. You worked hard to gain your father's attention."

"You complain about their toxicity and how they were narcissistic, how they only put their careers first, and that's what you're doing. You'll take my baby away from me if I don't marry you."

Those words sunk in.

They hurt.

And there it was. He was only marrying her because he was afraid of her leaving. He didn't love her. He just didn't want her to leave.

She should've known. She should've trusted her instinct. She should've kept her distance, but she was in love with him.

She'd never stopped loving him, but she wasn't going to marry him because of a sense of duty. She wasn't going to marry him because she was pregnant with their baby.

And she wasn't going to marry a man who, deep down, didn't trust her. Who didn't love her.

Tears stung her eyes. "I can't marry you, Calum. I won't marry you."

"You can't leave. Why do you want to leave?"

"And you just want to marry me to make me stay so that I won't leave you like your father left you!"

He took a step back, like she'd slapped him. She'd gone too far, but so had he.

She turned to leave. She had to get away from him. She couldn't be around him. As she walked to the door, there was a panic in the CT room.

Dr. Knox ran out. "George is crashing!"

She spun around on her heel and dashed for George. A resident had intubated and was doing chest compressions. She took over and Calum followed behind her.

Right now, she didn't have time to talk about the past. She didn't have time to think about her feelings, about her hurt, or the fact that she'd turned down the man she loved and always had loved.

She had a life to save.

Calum was crushed that Pearl had turned him down and he was so mad at himself for what he said. He regretted it the moment he said it, but she was going to leave again. She wasn't going to stay in San Francisco, and she was going to take their baby with her. He loved her. Why couldn't he say that?

He didn't want to lose either of them. And he

was shocked Pearl was pregnant again. With his child.

He was still processing it all. He couldn't quite believe it when he saw the lab report. He couldn't quite believe that Pearl was pregnant again.

And then the world came crashing down. She said no, he lashed out and George crashed.

He was angry at himself for saying those things to Pearl and he was angry that she had said those things to him, but she wasn't wrong.

He was terrified of losing her again.

He was terrified of her losing the baby and losing her.

Calum was ecstatic about the baby, but he wanted Pearl. It had always been Pearl and now he'd ruined it. He'd gotten so hotheaded and had wanted to stop her from leaving. He had tried to cage her and that was foolish.

And then George almost died.

Calum had just spent the last hour consulting the oncology team and the outlook was grim. Pearl was standing next to him as they observed George through the glass window of the intensive-care unit, but they hadn't said a word to each other. The tension between them was palpable. George's mother was by his bedside and

George was coming to. The ICU attendant had pulled out the breathing tube and George's vitals were stable.

For now.

So he and Pearl stood there, side by side.

He could sense that she was angry at him and he couldn't blame her.

He was angry at himself. Right now, though, they had to work together to save a life.

"So there's no choice," she said.

"No. He'll die if we continue this. It's too far gone."

Pearl nodded. "I'll break the news to him."

"I can do it."

She glared at him. "He's my patient. I will break the news to him. It's his dream that's being shattered. If anyone understands that, it's me."

"Really?" he asked. "How was your dream shattered?"

"I wanted our baby, too, you know. I was devastated when I lost it."

"So was I."

"I was grieving," she said.

"I was grieving, too, and you left me. Just like everyone else has. For that, I do blame you."

Her expression softened for a moment and then hardened again. "I have to talk to George."

Calum watched her walking into the ICU room, where George was. He looked away—he couldn't watch her do it.

It was killing him. His heart was breaking all over again and he didn't know how to change it. He was afraid of her leaving again, of the loss again, and he didn't know what to do.

You do, you know.

He walked away and pulled out his phone. There was one person he had to talk to. If he was ever going to figure this out, there was one person that he had to make things right with and that was Grayson Munro.

"Calum, I'm surprised to hear from you," his father said on the line.

"I'm wondering if you had a few minutes to spare for me. We need to talk."

There was a pause on the other end. "Of course. Can you meet me in thirty minutes? There's a coffee shop not far from the hospital, the Café au Lait."

"I know the place. Sure. I can meet you there."

"Good. I'll see you soon, Calum."

Calum ended the phone call. He looked back

once at Pearl speaking with George and he felt a pang of guilt. He wished he could've helped him more, but as Dr. Chin used to say, sometimes there was nothing more to do.

Sometimes things ended to stop the pain.

CHAPTER TWELVE

"I DON'T UNDERSTAND," George said quietly. "I thought this was a new, cutting-edge treatment."

"It is," Pearl stated. "Unfortunately, your cancer is highly aggressive and isn't responding to either chemotherapy or radiation. We have no other choice. To save your life, we have to take your leg."

"Then take it," George's mother said through tears holding hand.

"No, Mom!" George snapped. "I'm a grown man. You can't take my leg. I just got to the NFL. This can't be the end of my career!"

Pearl swallowed the lump in her throat. She was trying not to cry. "I'm sorry, George. There are no other alternatives. The cancer has infiltrated too far. You'll die if we don't take the leg. There are good options for prosthetics. Prosthetics that will help you run again."

"No. No, Doc. I'm sorry, but no." He shook his

head, angry, not that she could blame him. She was angry for him.

She was angry that she had to deliver this news to him.

She was angry at herself for being too scared to try and make a life with Calum work.

She was angry at herself for running away five years ago. She was angry that she had hurt and left Calum.

She was a fool.

"Baby, please see sense," George's mother said.

"No." George wouldn't look at them. "I won't do it."

"Can I talk to him alone?" Pearl asked.

George's mom nodded and left the intensive-care unit. It was just her and George now.

"George, you understand that you will die. This will kill you. You'll still have your leg, but you won't be able to play, the chemo will make you so ill and the surgery to take away the tumor will destroy your muscles. It'll make a mess of your leg."

George glanced at her.

She was getting through to him.

"I can't lose my leg, Doc."

"You'll lose your life if you don't," she said

gently. "You're young. Your whole life is ahead of you. The cancer hasn't spread above the knee. It hasn't spread anywhere else, but it will sooner rather than later, and the strongest chemo isn't stopping its progression. If you let Dr. Munro take the leg, you'll have your knee still and there are athletes that still play professional sports with a prosthetic. It'll take some time, some physiotherapy, but you can still run. You can still play and in the meantime, I know that your coach offered you a job as assistant coach. The Bridgers still want you, George. Even if it's just for your brains instead of your speed."

A half smile appeared on George's face. "It's been my dream, Doc. It's been my dream for as long as I can remember."

"It can still be your dream. Sure, it looks a bit different, but you can still have what you want. You can still do what you love."

And just those simple words, which were supposed to help ease George's mind, hit her like a ton of bricks and tears welled up in her eyes.

"Whoa, Doc, are you okay?" George asked.

"I'm fine. Actually, I'm pregnant so I'm slightly overemotional."

George grinned. "That's wonderful."

"It is, but here's the thing… I lost a baby five years ago. I swore I never wanted a family. I didn't have the best childhood, but then I got pregnant, and when I lost that baby I was terrified of this happening again, but it has and with the same man."

"It's Dr. Munro, isn't it?" George asked.

"How do you know?" Pearl asked, shocked.

"I know when people are in love. I don't just have strategizing smarts. I have to say I'm a bit jealous, Doc. You're a beautiful woman and I'm sorry that you were my doctor and that someone else got there first."

Pearl smiled. "I'm very flattered."

"You've been in love with him a long time."

"I have. I thought he blamed me for the loss of our baby, and I thought he was better off without me, but I was wrong."

George sighed. "Well, I guess I have no choice then."

"No choice?" she asked.

"I'll have the surgery, Doc. It's not how I planned it, but I want a chance to live and I want a chance to find a woman like you and fall in love, have a family. I'd be throwing an awful lot away because I was afraid of a change of plans, because I was afraid to take a chance."

She nodded. "Good. I'm glad, George. You almost died and you're too young. We take care of this and you go through physio, we can have you back in fighting form in a year or so."

"I'm tired of feeling like shit," George sighed. "Book the operating room and can you call my coach to come in. I want to strategize with him."

Pearl smiled. "Of course. I'll let Dr. Munro know your decision."

"Thanks, Doc."

Pearl nodded and left. She found George's mother in the hallway and she told her his decision. The woman thanked her for talking sense into George and gave her a hug, then headed back into George's room.

Pearl sighed. She had to find Calum. She had to let him know what was going on. She headed to the ICU charging station.

"Can you page Dr. Munro for me?" Pearl asked.

"I'm sorry, Dr. Henderson, he left for the day."

Pearl was stunned. "He left for the day?"

"Quite suddenly," the nurse said, like it was strange for Calum to leave abruptly.

"Thank you." Pearl frowned and walked away. It was unlike Calum to do something like that, not that she could blame him really.

She'd hurt him, but she was going to change that. She was tired of running. She was tired of hiding and worrying about how life changed in an instance. Even though she was scared she might lose this baby, even though she was scared that she would be a terrible mother and worried that a marriage would end up like her parents, she was done running.

She didn't know what the future held, but for the first time in her life, she knew that if he'd have her, her future included Calum.

And only Calum.

Calum found his father sitting alone in a corner table. He looked a bit tired and worn out, but that really didn't surprise him too much. His father was in his sixties and was still trying to burn the candle at both ends.

He perked up when Calum came in. Calum made an order at the counter and then went to sit down with his father.

"I'm glad you called, Calum," Grayson said.

"Are you?"

"I am."

"It's just…you never seemed to really care in the past."

Grayson frowned. "I know. I was too busy some of the time."

"All of the time," Calum stated. "You were busy all of the time, Father."

"Well, I'm glad you called me because I've been wanting to talk to you, as you know."

"And I wanted to speak with you, since you're an investor with the Bridgers."

"Oh?" his father asked, which of course made sense that as soon as Calum mentioned one of his father's investments, his interest piqued.

"Your linebacker, George. I can't save the leg. The cancer is too far gone and I have to amputate or he'll die."

His father didn't seem shocked. "That's awful to hear, but I'm aware that the coach made contingency plans, and the Bridgers are willing to pay for his recovery and prosthetic."

Calum was taken aback. "But you invested a lot in this young man. Don't you just want to get rid of him? Isn't he a drain?"

"He's smart," Grayson stated. "The coach feels like he's an asset and wants to keep him on the team. I support the rest of the owners and the coach on this."

Calum was shocked. "I'm impressed you're backing this."

"Of course. Sometimes you can't stop cancer. I hoped you would for the sake of the young man."

"Amputation will save his life."

"And that's good, because sometimes there are circumstances where the cancer is too far gone and there's no hope and you've realized that you've wasted your life being angry, chasing something so foolish that you really have nothing to show for it. You have money and power, but you really have nothing, especially when no one cares."

Calum's stomach twisted in a knot. "What're you saying?"

"I had a heart attack last year and I almost died. It made me realize how wrong I've been my whole life about my priorities. It's why I wanted to talk to you."

Calum couldn't believe what he was hearing. *He had a heart attack?*

And as he looked closer at his father he started to see how his father had thinned out and aged a bit more. He saw the signs that he had ignored before, because he'd brushed his father away so many times because his father had run from him.

Pearl had come back and he was trying to force her into an uncomfortable situation. All he could think about was his own grief, his own hurt. Yes, he'd been alone, but he never followed Pearl. He had never fought for what he wanted.

He had never fought for their love.

Calum had assumed Pearl was like everyone else in his life that left him.

He'd forgotten that his mom had tried to fight for his dad.

His mom had tried to fight until the end. Even though it was useless and his dad never came back, she had always hoped he would. Calum had always thought she was foolish for doing that, but he had done the same with Pearl. He waited for her, hoping she'd come back.

The only difference was Pearl came back, and in his own way he was trying to push her away, too.

"How are you doing now?" Calum asked calmly.

"I'm good. I'm taking care of myself and putting things right. I'm making amends."

"So you wanted to tell me this to seek sympathy?"

His father shook his head. "No. Just to say, I'm sorry. I loved your mother, but I didn't like to be pinned down. I didn't like the responsibility of you and your sister—I didn't want that job."

"It's too late to take up that job."

"I know, but I wanted you to know that I didn't fight hard enough for you. I don't want you to make my mistakes. Career isn't everything, money isn't everything, and I wish I had found that out sooner. I'm sorry, Calum. I'm sorry for what I did. I don't have to have your forgiveness, but I wanted you to know just the same."

Calum really didn't know how to take that, but he understood his father for the first time, probably in his entire life.

"I appreciate you telling me this. Have you told Sharon?" Calum asked, wondering about his sister, whom he hadn't heard from in years.

"I have. She thanked me and that was the end of that. I want you to know, you don't owe me anything for schooling. I held that over you because I didn't know any better. I thought it meant I could control you and keep you in my life, but I was wrong."

"Thank you." He was having a hard time processing all this information. "I don't think I can forgive you for what you did to Mom, but for me, you have my forgiveness. I'm just sorry that this didn't happen sooner and for that, it's my fault. I was so wrapped up in my career and you were reaching out to me. I hope you can accept my apology."

Grayson smiled. "Yes. Thank you. I do."

Calum finished his coffee and stood. "You can call me. You don't have to do this alone."

His dad smiled up at him weakly. "I will."

Calum nodded and left.

He had to find Pearl and talk to her. If she didn't want to marry him, then that was fine, but he was going to make things right. He wasn't going to let her leave again. The two of them were in this together and he was going to make it work however she needed it to work.

He loved Pearl.

He had never stopped loving her.

He was never going to stop loving her. No matter what happened next.

No matter how uncertain the future was.

CHAPTER THIRTEEN

CALUM FOUND PEARL in the intensive-care unit. She was sitting at the nursing station, her head in her hands.

"Hi. Sorry, I heard you were looking for me," he said breathlessly.

He'd run all the way back.

He wanted to see her and he wanted to take care of George. The cancer had to come out today. Both physically and metaphorically.

Pearl glanced up, her eyes full of tears. "Where were you?"

"What happened?" he asked.

"Nothing, I just…you know I get overemotional and I was thinking about what happened and how foolish I was."

"No. I was the foolish one." He glanced over his shoulder because he really didn't want an audience listening in. "Come on, let's go talk. There's an empty meeting room down the hall."

Pearl followed him and he shut the door.

Once they were alone, he turned around.

"I love you, Pearl."

She blinked a couple of times.

"What?"

"I love you. If you don't want to marry me, that's fine. You're right. I was trying to keep you with me by having you marry me. I was not willing to change and move with you. I didn't go after you. I was stubborn and hurt that you left me, like everyone else has done. I love you so much. I always have and if staying in your life means that we don't get married or I have to leave here, I will. I just want to be with you."

A tear slid down her cheek. "What if I lose this baby?"

"What if you don't?"

"I—I don't know. I guess, I'm too afraid of going through that pain again." She sighed. "I know why I lost our baby and I can take precautions this time, but there's no guarantee. I don't want to let you down again. I've let so many people down..."

"Who? Your parents? I think they let you down, just like my parents did, too. My mother spent her whole life pining after a man who didn't want to be pinned down and my father has spent his whole life trying to earn more money, but ultimately that didn't get them the happiness they sought. I'm happy when I'm with you. You coming back into my life gave me back my life."

"Yes. The same. I love you, Calum. I always have. There's been no one else in my life. I felt like I let you down the way that I've let my parents down. I blamed myself for losing the baby, for leaving you…"

Calum closed the gap between them. "You can never be a burden. You are my life and I haven't been living that life these past five years."

"I'm so sorry that I left you. I was in so much pain I felt I had to hide it. I'm so sorry. I wanted our baby so much. It broke me when I lost it and I didn't know how to let you in. I didn't know how to share the grief."

He brushed away the tears with his thumb. "When *we* lost it. We're in this together."

She smiled and nodded. "Right."

"I don't ever want to lose you again. If this doesn't work out, we'll adopt—or not. I don't care, I just want to be with you. I want a life with you."

There was a knock at the door.

Calum stepped back and opened it. A nurse was standing outside. "Dr. Henderson?"

"Yes," Pearl said, stepping forward and wiping her eyes.

"The patient is in the operating room, prepped and ready."

"We'll be down shortly."

The nurse nodded and Calum shut the door. "What's this all about?"

"No one knew where you went, other than you apparently left for the day. I paged you, but you didn't respond. George agreed to the amputation, but only if we do it today. His vitals are good and we need to get rid of that cancer."

"I'm glad he decided to proceed. I thought he was against it."

"He was, but we had a good talk and he helped me understand some things."

"What's that?"

"Life isn't always as planned, and dreams don't always pan out, but strength and resilience and adaptability are what matters." She walked past him. "Come on, let's go give George a second chance."

* * *

The surgery went smoothly and though Pearl was sad that Calum's new procedure couldn't save George's leg, George would still have a life. The chemotherapy and radiation was killing him as much as the cancer was.

And she remembered Dr. Chin's words, too, which Calum reminded her of, and that was that sometimes doing good could cause more harm and sometimes it was better to let things go. She used to think that applied to her dream of a family. Even though she swore she never wanted that, she really did.

Deep down, she did.

She wanted roots and she wanted a safe place.

She wanted a place to call home.

She wanted Calum and she wanted a family with him, whatever that consisted of. She wasn't terrified of having a toxic relationship with Calum. She was afraid of having a toxic existence without him.

George was getting a second chance at life and as Pearl worked with Calum to ensure that George had that chance, she realized that she was being given a second chance at life, too, and she wasn't going to squander it.

She was done running.

* * *

"George?" Pearl asked.

George was coming to in the postanesthesia recovery unit.

It had been a long surgery, but Pearl was glad that they were able to take his leg and leave a good enough stump, that when it healed, he would be able to get a prosthetic. With physiotherapy and training, George had a chance to run again.

For now, he would could use that keen eye and mind of his to strategize and train. On some level she wished that she could follow him and continue to be his doctor, but she missed her time in this hospital.

She missed San Francisco and, most of all, she missed Calum.

Pearl could see that now.

And this was her life. For the first time in a long time, she was going to start making the right decisions.

"George?" she asked gently again.

"Doc? Is it over?" he asked, murmuring.

"It is."

"How bad was it?" he asked.

"Dr. Munro did an excellent job. When the

stump heals you can be fitted with a state-of-the-art prosthetic, and with physiotherapy you can be running again."

George smiled, his eyes still closed. "And all the cancer is gone?"

"That's right. No more chemotherapy or radiation. It's going to take some time for your body to heal, George. I'm going to give marching orders to your coach and your mom. Your body has been through a lot, but you're going to live, George."

"Well, of course I am." He opened his eyes and smiled at her, his dark eyes twinkling. "With you as my doctor, of course I am."

She sighed. "I'm no longer working for the Bridgers."

He frowned. "I have to say I'm sad about that, Doc, but I get it. You're in love with Dr. Munro and with the baby you're doing what's right for your family."

"Exactly, but if that new doctor the Bridgers hire is a jerk…you can always come back to me."

George smiled, his eyes getting heavy again. "Thanks, Doc. Thank you and Dr. Munro for saving me, for giving me a second chance at life.

I was too pigheaded and stubborn to see that I was killing myself for nothing."

"You're welcome, George."

George drifted back to sleep under the effects of his anesthetic. She slipped out of the recovery unit and informed George's mom, and everyone else who was waiting to hear about him, the status of the surgery and that he was doing well.

After many hugs, she went in search of Calum. Their conversation had been cut short due to the surgery and there was more that she wanted to tell him.

She texted him and he texted back that he was in his office. She made her way to the other side of the hospital and found Calum waiting for her in his office. She slipped in and shut the door.

"How is George doing?" he asked.

"He's stable. He's doing well. I wanted to stay in the postanesthesia recovery unit until I made sure that he woke up and was okay. I told him that it will take time, but he should make a full recovery."

"We got all the cancer and I'm so pleased with that. He'll have a big adjustment, but you can take care of that as his physician."

"No, I can't."

Calum looked confused. "I don't understand?"

"I mean, I resigned." She worried her bottom lip, her heart racing.

His eyes widened. "What?"

"I'm no longer the team surgeon for the Bridgers." It felt weird to still say it out loud, but it also felt right.

"You loved that job. You were good at it."

She sighed. "I do love my work, but I didn't love that job. It was a means to escape. I did run, but I was afraid of having a toxic relationship with you. I didn't think that a relationship could work between two people who worked together, but being here in this hospital again, it reminded me of everything I gave up. The most important piece of that was you."

Calum smiled, his expression softening. "So what are you saying?"

"The chief of surgery said I had to clear it with the head of orthopedic surgery, but I would like to work here. If you could use another attending?"

"This is what you want?" he asked.

She grinned, nodding. "Yes. It is. I want to come home."

Calum stood up and took her in his arms. "I think that can be arranged."

"I want to stay in San Francisco. My life is here and I was a fool to think that I could run from it. I love you, Calum, and I'm glad that I get a second chance with you and I'm sorry that I wasn't there when you needed me most, when I needed you the most. I was just too lost in my own darkness to realize that."

"I love you, too, but I will say as your superior the moment the obstetrician puts you on bedrest you're done. No more surgeries!"

"I'm seeing the OB in the morning and we'll talk about what happened last time. There's no guarantee this one will stick. It's all risky." And it terrified her still. She was nervous.

"It's worth the risk." He tipped her chin and kissed her gently. "It's worth the risk to have you in my life. To have you stay with me."

"I love you." She kissed him again, deeper this time. "And in answer to your other question, yes."

He looked confused. "What other question?"

"Yes. I'll marry you. If you still want to get married?"

His eyes twinkled and he smiled. "I still want to marry you. How about Saturday?"

She laughed nervously. "The courts won't be open."

"Yeah, but Las Vegas is always open. We can fly down, get married. What do you say?"

"I think it's insane."

"Insanely good, right?" he teased. "So, what do you say?"

She kissed him again. "I say yes."

And he answered her, by kissing her and never letting her go.

EPILOGUE

One year later

"Did you tie the bolt down?" Pearl asked.

"Yes," Calum answered, stuck under the pine tree they had purchased at the lot and trying to adjust the tree in a very rickety stand. Max the sheepdog was under the tree, watching what Calum was doing and wagging his tail nonstop.

"It looks crooked."

He frowned at her briefly from under the tree. "That's not helpful."

She chuckled. "Well, I don't know… There was nothing wrong with a fake tree."

"Those are awful. This is Aidan's first Christmas and we're going to have a proper real tree."

"Did you grow up with real trees? I grew up with fake ones," she teased.

"Well, no. This is my first real tree, but I learned all about them before I decided on this."

"You educated yourself?" she asked.

"Of course."

Pearl rolled her eyes as Calum went back to work under the tree, cursing and muttering to himself. What he needed was a better tree stand, but he was happy with the one he had bought himself.

He'd just underestimated the size of the tree he'd purchased.

It was cute that he thought they needed a real tree for Aidan's first Christmas when Aidan was only three months old. Pearl glanced at him, sleeping soundly in his portable bassinet, totally unaware of the ministrations that his father was going through to make his first Christmas magical.

When it was already magical.

Aidan had been their miracle baby. The pregnancy had been a breeze. She'd gone into labor and Aidan was born on his due date, promptly and quickly.

She had a feeling that if she ever had another baby she wouldn't be so lucky. And he was the best baby there was, sleeping through the night, no colic. Calum liked to tease that he was an alien baby because he was just so perfect.

Pearl didn't know about the alien thing, but

she couldn't help but agree that he was perfect. Everyone doted on him and Derek, her godson, called himself honorary big brother. Derek was walking so well. He couldn't climb as well as he used to, but he was still active and Pearl was glad to have Derek in Aidan's life.

He was going to be a good influence. Although, Dianne still like to bring up that she thought it was a sore spot that she didn't get to go to their impromptu wedding in Vegas. However, Dianne and Jerome being Aidan's godparents more than made up for it.

After the wedding she moved into Calum's home and together, when she was feeling up to it, they finished off renovations. His little apartment inside the home was good enough for him, but Pearl had other plans for the large home.

The Bridgers had sent over a team onesie, personally delivered by George, who was managing so well with his prosthetic. When he had come over to see the baby, he was talking to her about training in the spring and that he was getting married to his old college sweetheart.

They'd gone their separate ways when he was drafted to the Bridgers because she didn't want to go to San Francisco and he had shut her out because of his cancer. George had been inspired by what Pearl and Calum had gone through, the moment he could travel again, he went to Philadelphia, found Reese and proposed right there and then.

Max barked and the sharp sound startled Aidan so he began to fuss.

Pearl scooped him up and held him close. He instantly stopped fussing and her heart soared with happiness. Aidan George Munro was the perfect child and she was so lucky to have him.

Her parents were distant and Calum's mother was gone, but Grayson was involved in his grandson's life, though Calum was still sorting through his emotions for his estranged father. Still, he didn't deny his son is grandfather. Aidan had enough people who weren't blood-related to make up a family and that was all that mattered.

Blood didn't make a family. Love did.

Max barked again.

"Max, you're not helping matters, buddy." Calum slid out from the tree. It was still leaning heavily on its side. He frowned. "I can do a surgery so intricate on delicate, brittle bones, surgeries that deal with nerves, and yet that blasted tree…"

Pearl laughed. "You need a bigger stand. Your eyeballs were bigger than the stand you had."

Calum nodded. "Yes. You may be right."

"What do you mean I may be right? I am right. Look at that thing."

He stood up and stretched. "Fine. You're right."

Calum put his arm around her and stared down at his son.

"I'll get a bigger stand in the morning," he said.

"Good." And as she said good Max stood up from under the tree and they both watched in amusement as the tree fell to its side again.

"You know, this reminds me of one of those cheesy Christmas movies where the dad over-estimates the ratio of tree and house."

Calum chuckled. "I will not be that dad."

"You have a blinding amount of lights outside the house. You are so that dad and trying to make a good old-fashioned, fun family Christmas."

"Fine. I am. We both haven't had really traditional Christmases. I wanted something Aidan would remember…even if he won't remember this." Calum picked up the tree and set it in a corner until he could get a new stand.

Pearl headed over to the large bay window, to

look out over the street and all the lights. Aidan was sleeping in her arms, but it didn't matter.

This time of year had never really mattered to her, until now.

Calum came up behind her. "I love you. Thank you for being my family."

"I love you, too. Thank you for being my family."

He kissed the top of her head, his arms around her and her arms around their son.

Now she understood what these holidays meant, because she had finally found her family. Even if it had been under her nose all this time.

She had found her family.

She had finally come home.

* * * * *

1	2	3	4	5	6	7	8	9	10		11	12	13	14	15
16	17	18	19	20	21	22	23	24	25		26	27	28	29	30
31	32	33	34	35	36	37	38	39	40		41	42	43	44	45
46	47	48	49	50	51	52	53	54	55		56	57	58	59	60
61	62	63	64	65	66	67	68	69	70		71	72	73	74	75
76	77	78	79	80	81	82	83	84	85		86	87	88	89	90
91	92	93	94	95	96	97	98	99	100						

101	102	103	104	105	106	107	108	109	110		111	112	113	114	115
116	117	118	119	120	121	122	123	124	125		126	127	128	129	130
131	132	133	134	135	136	137	138	139	140		141	142	143	144	145
146	147	148	149	150	151	152	153	154	155		156	157	158	159	160
161	162	163	164	165	166	167	168	169	170		171	172	173	174	175
176	177	178	179	180	181	182	183	184	185		186	187	188	189	190
191	192	193	194	195	196	197	198	199	200						

201	202	203	204	205	206	207	208	209	210		211	212	213	214	215
216	217	218	219	220	221	222	223	224	225		226	227	228	229	230
231	232	233	234	235	236	237	238	239	240		241	242	243	244	245
246	247	248	249	250	251	252	253	254	255		256	257	258	259	260
261	262	263	264	265	266	267	268	269	270		271	272	273	274	275
276	277	278	279	280	281	282	283	284	285		286	287	288	289	290
291	292	293	294	295	296	297	298	299	300						

301	302	303	304	305	306	307	308	309	310		311	312	313	314	315
316	317	318	319	320	321	322	323	324	325		326	327	328	329	330
331	332	333	334	335	336	337	338	339	340		341	342	343	344	345
346	347	348	349	350	351	352	353	354	355		356	357	358	359	360
361	362	363	364	365	366	367	368	369	370		371	372	373	374	375
376	377	378	379	380	381	382	383	384	385		386	387	388	389	390
391	392	393	394	395	396	397	398	399	400						

401	402	403	404	405	406	407	408	409	410		411	412	413	414	415
416	417	418	419	420	421	422	423	424	425		426	427	428	429	430
431	432	433	434	435	436	437	438	439	440		441	442	443	444	445
446	447	448	449	450	451	452	453	454	455		456	457	458	459	460
461	462	463	464	465	466	467	468	469	470		471	472	473	474	475
476	477	478	479	480	481	482	483	484	485		486	487	488	489	490
491	492	493	494	495	496	497	498	499	500						

M/c 3209

								900	901	902	903	904	905
906	907	908	909	910	911	912	913	914	915	916	917	918	919	920
921	922	923	924	925	926	927	928	929	930	931	932	933	934	935
936	937	938	939	940	941	942	943	944	945	946	947	948	949	950
951	952	953	954	955	956	957	958	959	960	961	962	963	964	965
966	967	968	969	970	971	972	973	974	975	976	977	978	979	980
981	982	983	984	985	986	987	988	989	990	991	992	993	994	995
996	997	998	999	1000										